MYSTERY LIGHTS AT BLUE HARBOUR

BUDGE WILSON

Cover by Ric Riordan

Scholastic Canada Ltd.

Scholastic Canada Ltd.
123 Newkirk Road, Richmond Hill, Ontario, Canada L4C 3G5

Scholastic Inc.
730 Broadway, New York, NY 10003, USA

Ashton Scholastic Pty Limited
PO Box 579, Gosford, NSW 2250, Australia

Ashton Scholastic Limited
Private Bag 1, Penrose, Auckland, New Zealand

Scholastic Publications Ltd.
Villiers House, Clarendon Avenue, Leamington Spa,
Warwickshire, CV32 5PR, UK

Canadian Cataloguing in Publication Data

Wilson, Budge
    Mystery lights at Blue Harbor

ISBN 0-590-71389-2

I. Title.

PS8595.I47M97 1987   jC813'.54   C87-093166-0
PZ7.W54My 1987

9 8 7 6 5   Printed in Canada   2 3 4 5/9
                    Manufactured by Webcom Limited

1880014075

To my sister Joan
and
her students
at Lakefield Elementary School

Contents

Chapter 1
Home again

"It seems like a million years," said Lorinda to James as they strolled along Elbow Beach.

"What does?" asked her brother, slurping his feet through the wet spongy sand at the edge of the water.

"Since we got back from Ontario. It's only been a month, but it's like forever."

"Yeah. I know."

The six months that Lorinda and James had spent in Ontario had been hard in a lot of ways. Though they'd had exciting adventures, and found that city life could be fun, there'd been loneliness and heartache, too. The best part had been making some wonderful new friends. They'd never forget Jon Jackson, the businessman they'd met on the plane. He suffered from airplane phobia and the kids had helped him cope with his fear. In return, he'd treated them to a wonderful day in Toronto.

Lorinda stopped walking and faced James.

"D'you miss it?" she said slowly, almost as though she were asking herself the same question.

James didn't answer right away. He looked at the white surf dancing over the blue water and at the reef in the distance beyond the Groaner buoy, where one huge rock stood above the surface of the sea at low tide. He couldn't imagine anything more beautiful. Still . . .

"Sort of," he said. "Half and half."

"What do you mean?"

"Well, I don't really want to be anywhere else but here. How could I? I love the sea and the boats. Besides, there's Fiona and Glynis, my very best *old* friends. And Jessie. And Mom and Dad. All the same . . . "

Lorinda chuckled. "It still sounds funny to hear you call them Mom and Dad, instead of Mummy and Daddy." She sighed. "Sometimes it seems like it's the only thing from Ontario that really rubbed off on us. All the rest sort of got blotted out when we left, except in our heads. Like Aunt Marian and Uncle Harry and the hockey team. And Sarah. I miss her so much I could die. Duncan and George are as great as ever — but I need a *girl* friend." She kicked a round stone ahead of her as she walked. "I need to talk girl stuff sometimes."

"Me too," said James, stooping down to pick up

a sand dollar. "Boy stuff, I mean. Like with Hank. He's a boy, you know."

Lorinda laughed. "So I noticed." Then she sobered. "If only they'd write us a postcard or something. Then we'd know they hadn't just dropped off the edge of the world. Or worse still, forgotten us."

"I guess," she added, "we just wish we could have a big piece of *there* dumped down *here*. At least we like everything around here." She looked towards the end of the beach and saw a solitary figure approaching them. "Or *almost* everything. There's always Reginald Corkum." Lorinda frowned as she remembered the birthday party Reginald had spoiled. The time he'd pulled a sock over his head and scared them all on the beach. The efforts he'd made to stop them buying a special vase for their mother last Christmas. And then she thought of James saying that maybe Reginald was only mean to *them* because they were mean to *him*. She'd even let him persuade her to invite Reginald to her next birthday party.

James seemed to pick up on her thoughts. "At least you didn't have to ask him to your birthday party like you promised," he grinned as Reginald came closer. "You had it while we were away."

"Saved by Ontario," smiled Lorinda. Then she frowned as she looked at Reginald's scowl. "Just as big a twerp as he was six months ago," she sighed. "Look at that happy face."

James glanced at Lorinda. "You don't exactly look like Mrs. Sunshine yourself, pal," he said. "You could maybe just say hi or something."

"Hi," growled Lorinda as Reginald glumphed by.

"Hi," replied Reginald, looking straight ahead, brows drawn together.

"There!" exclaimed Lorinda, looking over her shoulder. "I don't know why I try. That *hi* of mine sure got a great response."

James grinned again. "Your *hi* sounded just about as friendly as if you'd said *drop dead!* And that's what the poor guy would do if you ever smiled at him."

"Oh, well," said Lorinda as she took off her shoes and started wading in the cold water. She leapt out of the way as the wash from a wave rose extra high and soaked her jeans. "At least he doesn't get in my hair *all* the time, the way Mildred did in Peterborough."

They were both silent as they thought about Mildred.

"Really weird," mused James.

"What? Who?"

"Mildred," said James. "She was so mean to you, and at the same time she tried to turn you into her best friend — by trying to make everyone else your enemy."

"Someone should have taken her aside the day she was born and given her the recipe for making friends, if that's what she wanted. She never stopped making fun of me or of Nova Scotia the whole time I was there. Not my idea of how to win a popularity contest."

"No," agreed James.

As they walked past the huge boulder that everyone called Glynis' Thinking Rock, they saw all their Blue Harbour friends sitting on the sand — Duncan and Fiona MacDermid and George and Glynis Himmelman. They were leaning against the flat side of the rock with their bare legs stretched out in the sun.

"Hi!" yelled Lorinda as all thoughts of Ontario left her mind. "You having a big conference? Or what?"

"They look worried," said James, biting his thumbnail.

"Sit down," ordered Duncan. (Always the big boss, thought Fiona.) "We called for you, but your mum said you were gone."

"We were."

"Yeah. So I see. Well," Duncan continued, "it's time we had a talk. No one talks about it to us, because we're just kids."

"All the same," said George, "we *know*. We're not *blind*, for Pete's sake. We can see what's going on."

"Even us," said Glynis, who was six.

"Yup," said Fiona, who was almost seven.

"Something really peculiar is going on out there," muttered George.

Out where? Lorinda looked at James. She felt stupid and she didn't like the feeling. And left out, which was worse. Had the six months in Ontario made her and James unable to see something so obvious that even Glynis and Fiona knew about it? She hated to ask what they were talking about so she just muttered, "Hmm!"

James looked at his bitten fingernail.

"Guess you're talking about the lights," he said.

Lorinda turned so fast to look at him you could almost hear her neck snap. She waited.

"Yeah," said Duncan. "Right on. The lights."

"But look," warned George. "Let's not talk about it here. Can't tell who might be listening from behind the bluff. Let's all go blueberry picking at the Patch this afternoon. We can talk on the barrens and no one will hear us."

"Oh, darn!" exclaimed Lorinda, thumping her palm with her fist. "We promised to baby-sit Jessie this afternoon."

"Aw, please, Lorinda! Bring her!" begged

Glynis who hoped she would someday have a daughter exactly like Jessie. "You can just plunk her down on a rock and she'll fill her pail with berries. She'll probably fill it with lots of sticks and leaves too, but she'll have a good time while she's doing it. Please, Lorinda."

"Well, O.K. But don't you dare scare her. About the lights and all," she warned, trying to sound like she knew what she was talking about. "She's only three, y'know. And her ears are flapping the whole time. Remember how hard it was to keep her from telling about Mom's present last Christmas? I don't want to go through *that* again!" They all laughed.

"Don't worry," said Duncan. "We'll be really careful." Then he raised his arm like a schoolteacher. "O.K. then! This afternoon at the Patch at two o'clock. Everyone be there. Don't be late. We need to find out what each of us knows."

Like nothing, thought Lorinda ruefully as they headed for home and dinner. She felt a cold, nudging fear somewhere just above her belly button. "See you this aft'," she called to the other kids.

Chapter 2
Mystery lights

It was hot that afternoon on the blueberry barrens. There were no large trees on the Patch to cast any shade, and a hill stood between the kids and the windy coolness of the Bay. All around them were low bushes and rocks, small pale wildflowers, sweet smelling bayberry leaves. And blueberries by the tonne. It was hard not to start picking as soon as they got there. But after all, that wasn't the real reason they'd come.

"O.K., now," announced Duncan acting, as Fiona said later, like the President of National Fish or the Admiral of the Fleet. "Everyone sit down. You there, Lorinda, beside George. And the younger kids on the other side. When you're all settled, we can get started."

"I want to pee," announced Jessie.

"Omigosh, Duncan," gasped Lorinda, "we forgot about Jessie." She took her by the hand and led her behind a little knoll of rocks. Afterwards, she sat her down in the middle of a patch of blueberries, close enough that the kids could keep an eye on her but far enough away that she wouldn't be able to hear what they were saying. Then Lorinda handed her a sandpail. "Now pick!" she ordered. "If you fill your pail, I'll make you blueberry muffins tomorrow." But Jessie was already throwing berries into her pail — plunk, plink, plop. Lorinda could see that she wasn't going to be able to get out of making those muffins.

"C'mon! C'mon! Get a move on!" yelled Duncan.

"Oh, for Pete's sake, calm down," snapped Lorinda. "It isn't going to be the end of the world if I take two more minutes."

"Right!" mumbled Fiona through a mouth full of blueberries. Duncan raised his eyes towards the cloudless sky.

"Girls!" he lamented with a long sigh.

"It hasn't got anything to do with being girls," said Lorinda, tossing her long black hair over her shoulders. "It's got to do with not acting like everything's such a *crisis* all the time."

"Well," said Duncan, "I hate waiting. Mum always says it's such a waste of time, and it's true." They all fell silent, thinking about how Mrs. Mac-Dermid seemed to think life *was* a never-ending crisis. But nobody mentioned it.

"Besides," put in George, "there *is* a crisis. That's why we're here."

"A what?" said Glynis. "What's a crisis?"

"I kind of like that word," grinned George, "so I once looked it up in the dictionary — last Christmas when we were having that big crisis over the vase for Lorinda and James' mother."

"What did it say?" asked Glynis.

"It said, 'time of acute danger or difficulty.'"

Lorinda was dying to say, "And you mean to tell me this is a time of acute danger or difficulty?" But she didn't want to let on to anybody, not even to James, that she had no idea what everyone was talking about. After all, James was more than three years younger than she was.

"If it's so dangerous and difficult," frowned Glynis, "what makes it so cute?"

George slapped his legs and laughed and laughed. "Oh, Glynis," he roared, "wait'll I tell that to Mum and Dad!"

Glynis didn't even smile. She just held her blonde head up very high and said to Duncan, "O.K. Let's start talking about the crisis."

Maybe, thought Lorinda, if I keep really quiet and listen hard, I'll know as much as they do by the end of the afternoon.

"Got any suggestions, Lorinda?" asked George.

"Suggestions?" Lorinda spoke very slowly. "No . . . no, I don't think so. Not yet. I'd just like to do some real heavy thinking." Like about what on earth you're talking about, she added to herself.

"Well," said Duncan. "*I* have some suggestions."

"Of course," muttered Fiona who had some thoughts of her own tucked away.

"First of all, let's describe the lights very carefully," said Duncan. "And then we'll try to figure out how dangerous and difficult our crisis is."

"Or how cute," said Glynis, just to pester George.

George gave her his big brother look. "O.K.," he said, "we can all mention what we've noticed. For instance, the lights are sometimes white and sometimes colored — red and green."

But where? *Where?* Lorinda wondered how long it would be before someone mentioned that.

"They move around," added Duncan. "And they seem to be on the water, not on the opposite shore."

Ah. Lorinda felt she was getting somewhere.

"Between the Groaner and Grey Island, in fact," said George.

"And only on nights when there's no moon," added James. Lorinda stared at him. How could he know all that? There'd only been one moon since they'd returned home. And he was only seven-and-a-half. "I heard Mr. Hyson and Mr. Westhaver whispering about it," he went on, "one day when I was fishing off the Government Wharf. They were talking behind the freezer. They said that on foggy nights, when it's flat oil calm, you can even *hear* things."

"Like?" They all leaned forward and looked at James.

"Oh . . . voices. Stuff like that. Scraping sounds. Sometimes motors and noises like oars in their row locks. Splashing. They said it's real faint, and if you were the slightest bit deaf you'd never hear it. But Mr. Westhaver . . ."

"Yeah? Go on."

"Well, he's got real good ears. To listen to him, you'd think he could hear them breathing."

"Them?" This came from Fiona.

"Yep. Them. Whoever they are. Or *what*ever they are."

Then the suggestions started to come almost too fast for Duncan, who was writing things down on a pad on his knee.

"Lobster poachers."

"Or fisheries officers looking for them."

"Ghosts."

"Oh, *Glynis!*" George made a scornful noise through his nose.

Fiona spoke up. "Arnold used to say there was a pirate buried on Pony Island with a gold doubloon in each eye. And that you could sometimes see him on windy nights."

"Gold what?" asked James, who didn't mind admitting he didn't know everything.

"Gold doubloons," said George. "Old gold coins from the ancient pirate days."

"Could it be that?" whispered Fiona. "Something about that dead pirate?" She shivered as she thought about the doubloons shining in his eyes.

"I'll write it down," said Duncan. He'd promised his mother he'd try to be nice to Fiona because her gerbil had died the night before.

There were more suggestions.

"Maybe Russians."

"Spies."

"Spaceships."

"I've got a question," said George, thoughtfully picking berries off the bushes and dumping them into his tin. "Why is everybody being so quiet about it? When us kids say too much the parents shut us up. And the grown-ups almost never mention it unless they think no one's listening." He scratched his yellow head. "Why?"

"Easy!" said Duncan.

"O.K. then," said Lorinda, who felt she knew enough now to speak. George was so doggone smart in school that if *he* asked a question, it must be all right. "Why the big silence about it?"

Duncan thrust his face forward and made bug-eyes at her. "Because," — his eyes narrowed — "they're all *scared*." He almost shouted the word.

Glynis gasped.

"Who's scared?" called Jessie, standing up so she could hear better.

"Oh gosh, Duncan," sighed Lorinda. "You promised not to frighten her." She went over and led Jessie to another patch of berries a little farther away. "My goodness, Jessie," she said, giving her a little pat, "you'll soon have enough for those muffins."

"Who's scared?" repeated Jessie.

Lorinda did some fast thinking. "Maybe the berries," she grinned. "Because they're all getting picked."

Jessie laughed. "I'm gonna make them scareder and scareder," she said as she plunged her hands down among the leaves.

As Lorinda went slowly back to join the group, she thought, I know who's scared — a little bit, anyway. *Me.* If the grown-ups are scared, then I sure am too.

"Why?" she asked again when she'd returned to the others. They weren't sitting down anymore but were busy filling their bowls and pails with berries. "Why would grown-ups be scared?" What an awful thought *that* was. Lorinda figured that grown-ups were allowed to be frightened if things were really dangerous or terrible, like if there was a war or an outbreak of leprosy or an earthquake on its way. But why would they be scared about a bunch of lights?

George cleared his throat. "I have theories," he said.

"You have what?" asked Glynis.

"Theories. Ideas. Solutions." I bet he's going to end up Prime Minister or something, thought Lorinda.

"For instance," George went on, "if the lights come from space creatures, of course they're scared."

"Why?" said Fiona. "I thought E.T. was real cute."

George smiled like a wise and patient old man. "Not all creatures from space may be as cute as E.T. They might want to do a lot more complicated things than phone home."

"Like conquer us," warned Duncan. "Or take over the planet."

"With weird weapons."

"Laser beams."

"And computers that are way smarter than ours."

"With indestructible armour."

"And horns, maybe," said Glynis.

"So," went on George, "it could be that. They

may know a whole lot more than we do and be keeping it secret so we won't be scared, too."

"Well, *I* feel scared already," admitted Lorinda. "I don't like things I can't understand."

"Well, *I'm* not one *bit* scared," said Duncan. "Of course, I'm a *boy*." Just then a twig snapped behind him and he jumped right off the rock he was on, spilling his berries all over. "My gosh," he whispered, "if they really were space people they could be anywhere. Like under those bushes." He pointed behind him. "Or worse still, *invisible*."

"Well," said George, still sounding like the Prime Minister, "that's only one theory. Me, I think it's more likely an enemy fleet. Or our own ships looking for submarines lurking at the bottom of the Bay."

"What's lurking?" asked Glynis, whose pail was almost empty but whose lips were blue.

"Lurking is . . . O.K. . . . let's see." George bit his lip. "Skulking. Creeping around. Slithering here and there. Hiding. Getting ready for some awful attack."

"On *us*?" Fiona's eyes were round.

"Oh, not exactly on us," said George playing alleys with his blueberries on a flat rock. "We're not important enough. Just a little two-bit fishing village. More like on Halifax. To blow it up. It's a real important port. It blew up once when two ships bumped into each other. And it almost blew up a second time in the last World War. Maybe the submarines'd like to make a real job of it this time."

Lorinda forgot about wanting to look like she knew everything. "D'you mean Halifax really *blew up?*" she exclaimed. Where on earth did George learn these things? Twelve is old but not that old.

"Sure," said George. "A big hunk of it, anyway. One of the ship's anchors flew off and landed in Chocolate Lake, six kilometres away. One of the ships was full of explosives."

"Oh my heavens!" gasped Lorinda. Halifax was only forty kilometres by air from Blue Harbour.

Overhead, clouds were beginning to group together in large black clumps.

"Look up there," said Lorinda. "We might not have to worry about anything, not if we get struck by lightning first. It's starting to rain and we're sitting ducks on this bare hill. Listen. There's the first thunder."

"Or Halifax starting to blow up," said Duncan cheerfully, as a muffled boom was heard in the distance.

James bit his nail while they collected buckets and cups and sweaters and Jessie.

"I bet it's lobster poachers," he said.

"Another theory of mine," said George.

"That's nothing to scare a parent," scoffed Lorinda. "That's nothing new."

"It depends," said George, "on who's doing the poaching. They could be coming from a long way off and making a big business of it. Like thousands and thousands of dollars. When people are afraid of losing a lot of money, they can be mean. And *dangerous.*"

Lorinda had stuffed pieces of tissue in Jessie's ears so she wouldn't hear anything. Jessie kept poking at her ears.

"I know *I* wouldn't want to be the one to report them to the Inspectors," said George. "I might wake up one morning with my toes sticking out of a plot in Pine Point Cemetery."

Fiona shivered.

Then Duncan said, "And if that's the RCMP or the Coast Guard or the Inspectors out there, they could be pretty mad if us Harbour people got in the way of their investigations."

"Of their what?" asked Glynis.

George scratched his head. "Oh, I dunno, Glynis. Go home and look it up in the dictionary. I don't know *everything.*"

Darn near it, though, thought Lorinda. Maybe I'll marry George, she mused. If he gets to be Prime Minister, I could lead a campaign to let girls play hockey any place they wanted. Besides, he's handsome. She looked at him in surprise. How come she'd never noticed that before?

As the kids slopped home through the rain they got quieter and quieter. We're all scared, thought Lorinda. And no wonder! We don't understand what's going on, and we don't know how to stop it. What's worse, the grown-ups won't talk about it. There's nowhere to turn for help. She felt a cold shiver across the back of her shoulders.

When Lorinda, James and Jessie reached home, they hung their wet clothes up on the back porch and stepped into the warm dry kitchen.

"Good news!" announced Mrs. Dauphinee. "There's a whole pile of mail for you from Ontario. Well, maybe not a *pile*. Three letters. The names are on the envelopes. One for James from Hank —"

James grabbed it and his eyes shone.

"And one for Lorinda from Sarah Cohen."

Lorinda shut her eyes and hugged the letter. "At long long last!" she exclaimed.

"And another for Lorinda," continued Mrs. Dauphinee, "from someone called Mildred, I think. It's hard to make out the writing."

"Well," sighed Lorinda as she took the last letter from her mother, "if the pages of this one are stuck together my heart won't be broken!"

Then Jessie poked at her ears and pulled out

the tissue. "Sure sounded scary," she said cheerfully. "All that stuff you were talking about."

"What's that, dear?" asked Mrs. Dauphinee from the other side of the kitchen.

"Oh, nothing important, Mom," said Lorinda, scooping up Jessie and carrying her towards the stairs. As they went up, she spoke soothingly into Jessie's left ear. "*Nice* poachers. *Nice* enemy submarines. *Nice* spacemen. *Nice* explosions. *Nothing to worry about.* Eh, Jessie?"

Jessie's eyes were bright under her wet black curls. "I could hear what you were saying," she said. "Right through the tissue."

Lorinda marvelled at how well Jessie could speak compared to a few months ago. She'd learned an awful lot while she and James were away. Then she thought about just exactly what Jessie had said. Well, she reflected, maybe it doesn't matter. I have a feeling we're all going to be a whole lot more scared before this is over. And it'll be easier for her if she can talk about it.

Then she dumped Jessie down on the bed and took the letters out of her pocket. "Now," she said, "I'll read you Sarah's letter."

Chapter 3
Old friends — old enemies

Jessie sat up straight against the pillows and waited while Lorinda ripped open the envelope.

"Remember," said Lorinda before she started to read, "Sarah was my very best friend in Peterborough. She made me feel loved when I was homesick and nervous about Aunt Marian, and she stuck up for me when Mildred acted like such a nerd."

"What's a nerd?" asked Jessie.

Lorinda frowned. "A nerd is . . . well, I dunno. I guess you could say that a nerd is a creepy person."

"Creepy?"

"Oh Jessie! Gimme a break. I want to read my letter."

Jessie pressed her lips together.

Lorinda spread out the letter on her little white desk and began to read out loud.

Dear Lorinda,

I miss you so much. Peterborough isn't near as nice with you gone. All the boys say how are we going to win all the hockey games next year without Lorinda? I say how am I going to survive without my best friend?

Guess what? Jon Jackson sent me and Hank each a plane ticket. To go visit you in Nova Scotia. He hasn't got any kids to spend his money on, so he says it's fun for him. He checked with your Mom and Dad first to see if it was O.K., but he asked them not to tell you so that it would be a surprise.

(Lorinda let out a shriek. Then she read on.)

I thought I would faint I was so happy. Then guess what? I failed my math and have to get extra tutoring this summer. So I can't come. I could just die. Write me soon.

Your Ontario friend,

Sarah.

P.S. I wish you were here to help me with my math. Social Studies and Music are a breeze. But I think there's a hole in my head where the math is supposed to be.

Lorinda put her forehead right down on the desk and groaned aloud.

"Oh, *Jessie!*" she moaned. "It's so awful I'm gonna collapse!"

Suddenly Lorinda jumped up from the desk and tore downstairs to the kitchen. Waving the letter in the air, she yelled, "Listen everybody!"

Mr. Dauphinee looked in from the back porch

where he was fixing an old lamp. Mrs. Dauphinee came in from the pantry with bread dough sticking to her fingers. James looked up from the kitchen couch where he was lying on his back with his feet up on the wall, reading his letter.

"What?"

"What's the matter?"

"What's up?"

Lorinda held the side of her head and stared at the ceiling.

"It's the blackest day of the year," she announced. "Jon — you remember, the man on the plane who had airplane phobia . . ."

"What's phobia?" asked Jessie.

"It's being scared in a way you can't fix — not just by being brave. You have to go to a therapist or somebody to get cured. Anyway, Jon gave Sarah a plane ticket to come visit us and guess what? *She can't come*! I can't stand it! How could anything be so terrible?"

James looked up. His face was a mixture of sadness and glee. His brows were drawn together but he couldn't keep a wide grin off his face.

"Gee, Lorinda," he said. "Am I ever sorry. We coulda had such fun. Because . . . Hank's coming. Jon sent him a ticket, too."

Lorinda felt mixed up. She was glad for James

and happy for Hank, but in a way it made her feel even more sorry for herself.

"I'm jealous," she muttered.

"What did you say dear?" asked her mother.

"Oh never mind," sighed Lorinda. "I guess I'll get over it sometime. Maybe when I'm ninety. Gee whiz, though. Sarah could have helped us solve the mystery of the lights."

There was a heavy silence in the big kitchen. Then Jessie spoke up from the floor by the stove where she'd been patting Gretzky, Lorinda's big grey cat.

"Pretty scary," she said.

Mrs. Dauphinee acted as though nothing had happened. "That's a shame about Sarah, Lorinda," she said quickly, giving her a big hug, sticky hands and all. "But she can come another time. Maybe next year. Don't forget she's still got the ticket. It'll keep."

Lorinda perked up a little when she heard that. But she hadn't liked the way her mother had changed the subject the minute the lights had been mentioned. Or the way her father had turned around and gone right back out to the porch.

That night, after Jessie was asleep, Lorinda walked to the window and looked out over the Harbour to the Bay. To the east, the horizon seemed to blend into the open sea. It's so beautiful here, she thought, and I wish so much I could show it to Sarah — the beaches, the Patch, the Harbour and all the boats, the reefs with the giant waves breaking on them in a storm. And the beautiful sunsets we usually have. Not like tonight when it's so cloudy.

It was getting very dark now. She could barely see the outline of Pony Island.

Suddenly Lorinda stopped breathing. There they were. The lights. There weren't many and they weren't bright, but they were going on and off, sometimes disappearing altogether, then flickering like small flames in the darkness. Lorinda had learned enough Morse code in school to realize that the lights weren't saying anything. Or at least not anything *she* could understand.

She started breathing again and tiptoed across the hall to James' room. He was sound asleep but she shook him by the shoulder and whispered, "Wake up, James!" She put her hand over his mouth and added, "Don't make a sound — and come *quick!*"

When James looked out Lorinda's window, he didn't say a word for about two full minutes. Then he simply gasped, "Oh my gosh, Lorinda!"

All at once Lorinda was sick of all the secrecy. "Listen, James," she said. "I'm going down and just plain *ask* Mom and Dad what it's all about." Turning away from the window, she grabbed a sweater and marched down the stairs. Jessie slept on in her bed, but James followed her.

It was dark downstairs in the living room. But by the light from the open kitchen door, James and Lorinda could see their parents standing in front of the window. Mrs. Dauphinee was holding on tight to their father, who had an arm around her shoulders.

"Oh, Jim," their mother was saying, "I just wish it would stop. Or that we knew what it meant, even if it was awful."

"Don't worry, Lydia," said Mr. Dauphinee. "The RCMP say it's nothing. So do the Coast Guard. Mr. Hyson phoned up and asked. Mrs. Murphy wrote a letter and got back the same answer. But you know all that. So why worry?"

"Why worry, indeed!" Mrs. Dauphinee's voice sounded unsteady. "Of *course* they all say it's nothing! D'you really think they'd tell us if they knew what it was all about? But," — and here Mrs. Dauphinee began to sound stronger — "if one particular part of the Bay is flickering with lights night after moonless night, nobody's going to tell *me* that it's just nothing. Of *course* it's something! But *what?*" She paused for a moment. "I just hope the kids don't get frightened. Did you hear what they said this afternoon? We've got to be really careful not to talk about it. We've just got to pretend that everything's normal."

"Well, everything's *not* normal!" This was Lorinda speaking, and Mr. and Mrs. Dauphinee turned around so fast they almost knocked one another over. "And what's more, we all *are* scared, so you might as well try to put up with that too. So how be we *talk* about it? I bet there isn't a single soul in Blue Harbour — except maybe Gretzky," she said, as the cat unfolded himself and came over to lean his head against her leg, "who doesn't know about those lights. So why pretend they're not there? It's just *stupid*."

Then Mr. Dauphinee went and turned on the lights and they all sat down in the living room in their night clothes.

"No," he said slowly, "it's not stupid. It's sensible. If there really is anything at all dangerous going on out there, it's wise to keep our heads hauled in a little. No one goes out in a rowboat to chase a whale or goes swimming with a shark. And unless you really know what you're doing and why, it also makes sense to steer clear of dangerous people or mysterious things."

Mr. Dauphinee sighed. Then he got up and started walking around the room, picking things up off tables and putting them down, glancing out the window and then away from it, fiddling with his pajama buttons. At last he spoke.

"Look, kids," he said, "we didn't want to scare

you with any of this stuff. But it seems you're scared anyway. So I guess Lorinda is right when she says it's better to talk about it — among *ourselves.*"

"Otherwise," broke in James, "we'll just keep it all inside and either get grumpy or else bust."

"Well," went on Mr. Dauphinee, "your mother's probably right. It's hard to believe the RCMP and the Coast Guard don't know what's going on. You can't have everyone up and down the shore calling them and writing letters without them going out and having a good hard look. Or maybe it's even *them* out there. Either way you look at it, they don't *want* us to know anything else. It's like they're telling us to put up with it all and shut up about it. Which," he concluded, as he sat down again, "is what I think we should do. Because there's got to be a reason."

Lorinda and James listened to all this, and at the end they couldn't think of a thing to say. It all seemed to make some kind of sense, but at the same time, Mr. Dauphinee's speech made them worry even more.

"Hey," said James, who had a way of solving things, even if it were done backwards, "what did Mildred say in her letter?"

"Yes!" exclaimed Mrs. Dauphinee, looking relieved. "Is that the girl in Peterborough who was, well, sort of . . ." Her voice trailed off.

"Yes," said Lorinda. "The nerd." She rushed upstairs and got the envelope. "I forgot all about it," she said when she returned. "I guess I didn't think the world would come to an end if I didn't hear her news." She opened the envelope and started to read the letter to them.

Dear Lorinda,

I've decided to come and visit you. Aren't you glad?

Lorinda looked up from the letter and growled.

"Oh no, Mildred! You're *not* coming to visit me! And no siree, I'm *not* glad!"

"But Lorinda!" exclaimed Mrs. Dauphinee. "What can you do? You can't just tell a friend not to come!"

"Well," said Lorinda, "to begin with, she's not what I'd call a friend. Beside her, a barracuda looks like a real fun pal. And yes. I *can* tell her not to come. I can write her and tell her I have measles, or that the house burned down, or that Pony Island turned out to be volcanic and erupted, burying the entire village of Blue Harbour under a sea of molten lava."

"Better finish the letter," interrupted James.

Lorinda picked it up again and started to read it to herself. Suddenly she stopped reading and stood straight up, swatting the side of her face with the flat of her hand.

"Oh my gosh!" she breathed. "I can't believe it. No matter what's going on with those lights out on the Bay, it can't be half as bad as what's about to happen to the Dauphinees. Mildred is going to arrive at Halifax International Airport *tomorrow morning* at 10:40, and we're supposed to be there to meet her. And she's going to stay for a *month*."

"Oh well," said Mrs. Dauphinee. "One month isn't so long."

"Mom," said Lorinda, her arms hanging loose at her sides, "being cooped up with Mildred for a month could seem like *forever*."

Chapter 4
Hank and Mildred

The next morning Lorinda's bedroom window looked like an empty TV screen. There was so much fog that you couldn't see even as far as the Government Wharf. The whole world was grey.

"Oh, great!" sighed Lorinda out loud. "Guaranteed to make Mildred even more cheerful than usual." She threw on her jeans and T-shirt and raced downstairs.

"Lorinda," said her mother, "don't look so miserable. When you're as old as I am, you'll know that a month is just nothing."

"Well," muttered Lorinda, "I'm *not* as old as you are, and a month is a great big huge something. At least Hank is coming on the same plane. That'll maybe dilute Mildred a bit."

"Get a move on, troops!" yelled Mr. Dauphinee from the back porch where he was still working on the lamp switch. "The taxi leaves for the airport in ten minutes!"

Some taxi, thought Lorinda, glancing out the

kitchen window at the Dauphinee truck. She thought about Mildred's father's car — black, shiny, and replaced every year. Imagine having a doctor for a father. Florida every Christmas holidays, and an allowance so big Mildred probably had trouble carrying her wallet around.

Lorinda caught a glimpse of herself in the kitchen mirror as she took her dishes over to the sink. She was shocked by her pinched, cross face. Leaning forward, she spoke to her reflection.

"You just pull up your socks, Lorinda Dauphinee!" she snapped. "No Mildred is gonna wreck your August. She can just fit in and be nice, or she can turn around and go home. And who wants an old doctor for a father! They're always out somewhere delivering babies or taking out tonsils or stitching up cuts. Mildred was always complaining because her dad was never home." She could see her own father in the mirror, out on the back porch patiently struggling with the lamp. "I like my father being just exactly what he is." She went out to the porch where he sat, and kissed him on the top of his head.

"Getting a little bit bald," she announced, "but otherwise nice."

He chuckled and looked up at her. "Getting a little bit rude," he said, "but otherwise nice."

*   *   *

They reached the Halifax airport with only ten minutes to spare. At exactly 10:40 the announcement came over the loudspeaker: "Flight number 152 arriving from Toronto. Passengers may be met at the baggage retrieval area." In spite of herself, Lorinda felt a slight stirring of excitement. Maybe this time Mildred would be different. It would be fun to have a girlfriend her own age in Blue Harbour. Glynis and Fiona often played with her, but they were much younger than she was.

When she saw Mildred and Hank sailing down the escalator, Lorinda felt as though she were back in Ontario. It just seemed so normal to see Hank's friendly wide-open face, his untidy hair, his grubby clothes. He was waving both arms and yelling, "Hi!" over and over again. Beside him, Mildred was standing sedately, both hands clasping her Air Canada bag, her hair all curled up and tidy, her hot pink stirrup pants smooth as glass, her white blouse starched and frilly, the expression on her face unreadable.

"Oh boy," murmured Lorinda. "Give me strength." She stared down at her own patched jeans and her old T-shirt, the one with "Herring Choker" printed on it in big letters.

Aloud, she shouted, "Hi, guys!" and rushed forward to hug them both. "Welcome to God's Country," she said.

Mildred seemed shy and silent. Well, thought Lorinda, maybe she left her tongue back home. Or maybe her mother told her to shut up unless she had something nice to say.

But it turned out that Mildred had a voice after all. When they got to the truck, James and Hank scrambled into the back and leaned against the old cushions near the cab, hauling a rug up over their legs. "It was thirty degrees in the shade when we left," said Hank. "Boy, is it ever neat not to be lathered up all the time."

That was when Mildred asked, "Are we going home in *that*?" Her eyes looked almost frightened.

"Yes," said Lorinda, "we're going home in *that*. It happens to be our car. But you and I'll be driving up front with Dad. It's not as much fun, but it'll keep your pants clean." I resolve, thought Lorinda in grim silence, to be nice till three o'clock tomorrow afternoon. That will leave just seven hundred and twenty hours to go before she leaves. Lorinda was good at arithmetic.

When they got in the cab, Lorinda took a deep breath and said, "Your blouse is pretty."

Mildred fingered the ruffles around her neck and patted the sleeves. "Yes," she said. "It was a going away gift from my dad. He said it would help make me feel civilized while I was living in a fishing village."

Lorinda stared at her. "Oh he did, did he?" she said through her teeth.

"Yes," agreed Mildred. "He said that the whole trip would be a valuable sociological experience for me. You know what that means, of course."

"Of course," said Lorinda, who had not the ghost of an idea what Mildred was talking about.

"My goodness!" exclaimed Mildred after a while, craning her neck to see above the hood. "Isn't there anything in this province except trees? We've been driving through Christmas trees for twenty minutes. Don't you have any big cities or anything? Or even farms?"

Mr. Dauphinee cleared his throat. "This road by-passes Halifax and Dartmouth," he said. "Right over yonder, beyond that hill, are the two biggest cities in Nova Scotia."

"Bigger by *far* than Peterborough," said Lorinda, and hoped this wasn't breaking her resolution. "And we've got other things. Beaches and lakes and islands and sea. Besides, I like Christmas trees."

"Well yes," hesitated Mildred, fiddling with one of her curls, "I suppose so. If it happens to be Christmas. Of course we have lots of country like this up north, but that's hunting and fishing country."

"Could be some real live humans live up there too," put in Mr. Dauphinee. "Just like us." He grinned and patted her on the knee. "You'll get used to it," he said, chuckling. "Maybe after a month, even the fog will start looking good."

Lorinda looked out the window at the scrubby spruce trees and at all the grey nothingness behind them. Then she glanced at Mildred. Suddenly she felt sorry for her. She remembered back to last January when she'd felt so lonely and uneasy in a new place among strange people. To someone not used to it, all that fog might almost be scary.

"He wants it fine for tomorrow," said Lorinda, keeping her voice cheerful.

"Who wants what?" asked Mildred, mystified.

"The Weatherman," explained Mr. Dauphinee. "That's just an expression we have down here. It means the weather prediction is for fine weather."

"Well, then," said Mildred, giving a shaky little laugh, "*I* want it fine for tomorrow too," and they all laughed.

When they reached Blue Harbour, an hour and a half later, Mr. Dauphinee drove the truck into the driveway and they all piled out — Hank and James laughing and talking, Mildred and Lorinda quiet but polite.

"What a swell house!" exclaimed Hank, ignoring the sagging back veranda. "I never seen an orange house before. Ever *neat!*"

Mrs. Dauphinee was at the door to greet them.

"Welcome to Blue Harbour, kids!" she said, holding out her arms wide. "Did you have a nice ride in the airplane?"

"Yes, *ma'am!*" cried Hank. "We had a meal on a tray with holes for all the different things we ate. And little forks and knives wrapped up in a package. And free coke."

"How about you, Mildred?" asked Mrs. Dauphinee. "Let me take your suitcase. My, it's heavy!"

Mildred screwed up her nose. "They served fish. I can't stand fish." Mr. and Mrs. Dauphinee looked at one another, eyebrows raised.

Lorinda coughed nervously. "Oh well," she said, as they climbed the stairs, "you'll like the way Mom cooks it. Or you'd better like it, anyway. We have fish five times a week."

"Five times a *week*?"

"Yeah. Two days we have meat. For a treat."

Mildred's face looked all closed up under her fat curls. "Are there gonna be seven of us all living in this tiny little house?"

"Sure," said Lorinda, thinking about the twenty-seven hours she'd vowed to be nice. "Easy. Hank will sleep in James' room. We borrowed a cot from the Himmelmans." Then she added, "They've got lots of money and furniture and not many kids."

"But what about us?" puffed Mildred as she

lugged her Air Canada bag up the stairs. "You and me?"

"You and me and Jessie will sleep in here," said Lorinda, proudly opening the door to her bedroom.

"Boo!" shrieked Jessie, jumping out from behind the door.

"That's Jessie," said Lorinda, scooping her up and giving her a big hug. "This used to be my room before Jessie was born. Now we both own it. Jessie and I'll sleep in the big bed, and you can have Jessie's."

"You mean you're gonna sleep with *her*?"

Lorinda hugged Jessie harder. "Yes siree!" she said firmly. "She's kind of squirmy, but she doesn't snore. And she's way better to hug on cold nights than a teddy bear."

Mildred was looking all around the room. Lorinda looked, too, as though for the first time. Peeling paint, she noted, remembering Mildred's perfect pink bedroom with its ruffled curtains and matching bedspread. Lorinda's bed, a spool bed painted bright blue, had a big patchwork quilt on it — made by her grandmother. It was faded from many washings and worn-out from being sat on, and from all the games of Monopoly that had been played on it. Jessie had a little brown metal bed. The curtains on the window were blue and white checks, and there were hooked mats on the floor.

The floor itself was old wide boards, uneven and sometimes splintery, painted navy blue. The walls were covered with pictures, pennants, some scribbly drawings by Jessie, field day ribbons, a mirror with a wavy glass, a huge poster of the CN Tower from Lorinda's trip to Toronto, and a big oval picture of her great-great-grandmother in a high-necked collar with her hair piled on top of her head.

"Well," sighed Mildred. "It's sure *different*."

"Yes," said Lorinda stiffly. "I suppose it is. Different can be good, you know."

"That's sort of what Mom said," murmured Mildred. "She said that even if life down here was pretty peculiar, at least it would be something to talk about afterwards." Lorinda could imagine Mildred — could actually *see* her — in the playground of Duke of York School, telling everyone about the broken veranda and the peeling paint in Lorinda's bedroom. And about all the fish she'd had to eat.

"Dinner, kids!" yelled Mrs. Dauphinee from downstairs. "Wash up and get down here!"

There were fish patties for dinner. Lorinda watched Mildred take one small forkful then push the rest aside. Maybe she'll starve to death, she thought savagely. Realizing that this could be complicated or messy, she added to herself, maybe she'll hate the food so much she'll just up and leave. But no such luck. After Mildred tasted Mrs. Dauphinee's homemade brown bread, she had six slices. Lorinda counted. Hank ate everything, forgetting to use his fork sometimes, stuffing it all in as though he were *really* starving. Maybe he is, thought Lorinda, remembering the shabby little house he lived in with his seven sisters and brothers. With his mouth full, he was talking to Mrs. Dauphinee. "I never had such a nice meal," he said, licking his fingers before wiping them on his pants. Then he added, "No. That's not true. I ate real good dinners at Aunt Marian's, but she scared me so much I couldn't swallow right. I wish I could stay here a million years."

I think he almost means that, thought Lorinda.

Jessie got off her chair and walked over to Hank. "I love Hank," she said, and laid her cheek against his leg.

*   *   *

The next meal was late, so it was almost dark by the time Lorinda and James finished the dishes. "Your turn tomorrow," said James to Mildred and Hank. "We're just being nice because it's your first night. So don't get too used to being lazy."

"You mean I'll be doing the dishes with *him*?" said Mildred, eyebrows in a knot. She was staring at his dirty fingernails.

"Yes," snapped Lorinda. And I wish, she

thought, that Hank really did have germs, so you'd catch bubonic plague. Or *leprosy*. Then she realized she was close to breaking her resolution, and said to her father, "Hey Dad. Let's take them down to the Government Wharf where they can hear the water and smell the tar. We can show them the traps too." She turned to Mildred. "It's too foggy to see very far, but there's a lot more to a fishing village than seeing. At night, it's all sort of still and mysterious."

Mrs. Dauphinee was putting Jessie to bed, so the five others grabbed sweaters and walked down to the Government Wharf. It was brightly lit in the darkness. The fog formed halos around the lights and made the edges of things soft and ghostly. They looked at the giant pulleys for hoisting tuna.

"Some tuna weigh over 300 kilos," said James.

"You wouldn't kid me, wouldja?" marvelled Hank. "Them tins are so little."

"That's about 299 more kilos of fish than *I'd* want to see," announced Mildred.

"Their teeth are real small, but they must have two million of them," Lorinda told Hank, adding, "Down here we call them albacore."

Hank hugged himself and groaned out loud. "Ohhhh! I'll *kill* myself if I don't get to see one," he said.

Then they looked at the coils of rope and the colored fish boxes and the piles of lobster traps.

41

They smelled the seaweed and the fish and the tar, and Lorinda breathed it in like a rare perfume.

"Phew!" sniffed Mildred.

"Wait a spell," said Mr. Dauphinee in his slow, kind voice. "You may get to like it. And listen to the sounds. That lapping noise is the tide sloshing around the timbers under the wharf, and that's the Groaner you hear. It's our closest buoy."

They all stood still to listen. The Groaner's "mmmmmm*uh*" sound came through the fog in a long grunt.

Then, quite nearby, on a neighboring wharf — or so it seemed — they heard an odd moaning. As they stopped breathing to listen, other sounds carried over the water from far out at sea — a low whistle, the thunk of oars, splashing water, voices so distant you couldn't make out the words.

"Time for bed!" announced Mr. Dauphinee suddenly. He spoke cheerfully, and no one but Lorinda and James could have guessed what he was feeling. As they passed the neighboring wharf, he slipped down to check the gear. "Seems O.K.," he said when he came back. But Lorinda could hear scurrying sounds in the bushes ahead of them. By the time they reached home, she wasn't upset any more about the long month ahead with Mildred. She had more important things to worry about.

Chapter 5
Lost at sea!

"So!"

Lorinda opened her eyes to see Mildred standing in front of the window.

"So?" she mumbled in reply, her voice fuzzy.

"So this is what your Weatherman calls a fine day."

Lorinda rubbed her eyes and stretched. What a way to wake up! It made all the hours left till three o'clock seem never-ending. How was she ever going to keep her resolution? "Being nice sure is one awful strain," she muttered to herself.

"What?"

"Oh, nothing important. About the fog. Sometimes the Weatherman makes a mistake. Never mind. It can't go on forever." She tried not to think of the summer of 1967, when they had eighty-five days of fog out of ninety-two. She hadn't even been born then — fortunately! — but her parents still talked about it.

"What do the kids around here *do* when it's

foggy? My gosh, if you played baseball and anyone hit a home run, you'd never find the ball."

"We'll find something nice to do," said Lorinda, her voice tight. "James and Hank are going off with Dad to collect roots, and probably Fiona and Glynis'll go too. But I don't expect that's exciting enough for you." She tried to keep her voice even, but she knew she was saying things that didn't fit in with her resolution.

"To collect *what?*"

"Roots of trees. For the bent part in a lobster trap. It's fun looking for them, and Mom always packs a swell picnic."

"A picnic in the fog?"

"Yes."

"*Really?*"

"Yes, really. We even have picnics in the snow in the winter when we go looking for Christmas trees or firewood."

"At home it's really sunny and hot," sighed Mildred, staring at the grey window and hugging her sweater around her.

Too hot, thought Lorinda, remembering the awful heat wave in June. But she figured she could wait to say that until after three.

"C'mon," she said, springing out of bed. "Let's eat. Then you'll feel more cheerful." Like heck, she thought. "I can smell bacon cooking. I could eat a whole package of it this morning."

They were just finishing off their breakfast when Duncan and George arrived at the back door. Duncan had freckles sprinkled all around his broad grin, and hair that looked even redder than usual against the grey of the fog. George's blond hair was just like Glynis', only short, and his blueberry eyes were both serious and friendly.

"We're jiggin' for mackerel this morning," said Duncan. "Wanna come?"

"Your friend might like it better than sitting around in the fog," said George.

Lorinda grinned. "Thanks, guys," she said. "This is Mildred. Mildred, these are my best friends, Duncan and George."

"Hi," said Mildred, looking hard at George, who was very handsome. "What's jigging for mackerel? Is it hard?"

"Oh, it's real easy," laughed Duncan. "You just bait your line, and then jig it up and down over the edge of the boat till you get a bite. Then you haul in the fish."

"Then your mum cooks it all up for supper," added George. "Or, if you catch enough, you go over and sell it at the Government Wharf."

"Wow!" exclaimed Mildred.

Mention money, mused Lorinda, and she perks

right up. But Lorinda cheered up too. Stick Mildred in a boat and maybe she wouldn't be such a pain. Add Duncan and George, and perhaps Lorinda could even forget Mildred was there.

"C'mon, Mildred," she said, grabbing her dishes and piling them in the sink. "Get a move on. The fish are all out there just sitting around waiting for us."

When they were upstairs, Lorinda said, "Better put on something grubby. Those pink pants'll never survive a fish jig."

"I don't *have* anything grubby. Just some jeans. *New* ones."

"O.K. That'll be fine. They won't look new for long, and then you'll fit right in with the rest of us. Put 'em on, and grab a warm sweater. It's cold out there. Even on a hot day."

"Is George ever cute!" breathed Mildred, touching her hair.

Lorinda gave her a sharp look. "For Pete's sake, Mildred! You're only eleven years old."

"So?"

"So never mind. Let's go. You can pick up a pair of boots on the back porch. We keep extras for guests."

"Why?"

"Otherwise they spend their whole visit sitting around drying out their shoes."

Mrs. Dauphinee stood at the door as they got ready to leave.

"Now listen to me," she announced, barring the doorway. "You don't put one foot out this door unless you promise to keep in sight of the shore. *All the time. Every minute.*" Mrs. Dauphinee's gentle face looked fierce. "A few metres can sometimes make the difference between being safe and being lost. And if you get lost in the Bay today, you could be halfway to Spain before anyone found you. Mind, now!" She moved away from the door, and Lorinda kissed her cheek. Mrs. Dauphinee was short and Lorinda was tall, so they were almost the same height.

"Don't worry, Mom," she said. "We're not that stupid. We promise."

*   *   *

Down by Mr. Coolen's wharf, the kids climbed the ladder into Mr. Hyson's green flat and put their fishing gear on the stern seat. Lorinda and Mildred sat down as Duncan and George each took an oar.

"What's the matter?" said Mildred to George. "Can't you row the boat by yourself?"

Boy, she really is strange, Lorinda thought to herself. She always wanted me to be her friend in Peterborough, but she never stopped bugging me. Or making me look awful in front of people. And here she is doing the same thing to George, when it's obvious she's got a crush on him. Lorinda scratched her head and frowned. It's like she wants to wreck people in the eyes of their friends, so she can have them all to herself.

"Come on over here and try it yourself," said George to Mildred, moving into the middle of the wide seat to make room for her. When Mildred tried to row, she could barely move the oar. It just rose a few centimetres off the surface of the water, then splashed back in. Mildred nearly fell over backwards.

"Want to row now?" asked George, with a gleam in his eye.

"My *heavens!*" crooned Mildred. "You must be so *strong!*" George tried to keep his face blank, but you could see he was pleased. Lorinda could feel a hard knot forming in the centre of her stomach.

"Hey, look!" she whispered suddenly. "Look who's watching from Mr. Coolen's wharf." And there was Reginald Corkum, sticking out his tongue and yelling.

"Hope you catch a sculpin! Hope you sink!"

"And I was just thinking," said Lorinda, "that maybe we should ask him to come. Well," she chuckled, "he sure fixed *that!*"

Keeping their eyes on shore, to make sure it didn't disappear, they worked their way out towards

Pony Island. When they started their jigging, they were all quiet for a while. Then Duncan felt a bite, and before long he had hauled a squirming mackerel into the boat. Mildred screamed, "It's wiggly and awful! Get it away from me!"

"Calm yourself, Mildred," said Lorinda, who knew that neither George nor Duncan expected girls to be weak or scared. "Take a look at him. He's beautiful. Look at the pretty pattern on his back. Ever gorgeous. And wait'll you taste one."

When Mildred finally got a bite she nearly fell out of the boat. She was that excited. She hauled in her line so fast that it got all tangled up. The big fat mackerel on the end of it thrashed around like a mad thing on the bottom of the boat. While George took the fish off the hook for her, Mildred stared and stared at it.

"I caught it!" she marvelled. "I really and truly caught it. All by myself." Gingerly she reached forward and placed her index finger on its slippery back. The fish moved slightly, but Mildred didn't scream. "So smooth!" she whispered.

Lorinda watched her, and her heart lifted a little. Maybe she could make it to three o'clock after all. Or maybe right to the end of the month.

Then they all stopped admiring Mildred's fish, because George suddenly cried, "Look!" Lorinda's chest tightened as she raised her head. There was no sign of land at all. It was exactly as though they were in the middle of a perfectly round, fuzzy-edged pond. On all sides, and above them, too, was a wall of grey.

"Now what?" she said.

Duncan, as usual, was full of plans. "We row till we hit something."

George, as usual, was thinking. "Yeah," he put in, "and by nightfall we end up somewhere on the other side of Eastern Island." Everyone knew that once you got beyond Eastern Island there was nothing between you and Europe. Just 5 000 kilometres of Atlantic Ocean.

Mildred's lower lip trembled. "Today's my mother's birthday," she said.

Lorinda reached over and patted her on the shoulder. "Buck up, kiddo," she said kindly. "I vote for us all letting go with a big yell. One, two, three, *go!*"

They all joined in a long loud yell, and then they waited. Silence — and the far-off cry of one lone seagull.

"We could listen for sounds," suggested George. "Like if we hear the Groaner, we'll know sort of where we might be." But when they listened, it was hard to tell if the buoy's long grunt came from behind or beside them. It was so calm that there wasn't even any sound of surf — on the islands or on the reefs or on the shore.

Lorinda shivered. She was really worried about her mother.

"If I didn't have to worry about Mummy worrying," she said, using her old name for her mother without thinking, "I wouldn't mind so much. The tide's going out, but we can't have gone *that* far, because there's no wind."

"I know," frowned Duncan. "Mum'll be having ten fits. She's all alone in the shop. Dad's gone to Bridgewater for the day."

George didn't say anything. He was just sitting there thinking.

"We could look for the sun," he said at last, "But there isn't any. Not that you can see through this fog, anyway. The men aren't out fishing today, so we can't expect to be rescued by mistake. We can't hear any sounds at all, so that's no help. If we start rowing, we may go in the wrong direction. Besides, we'd get tired and maybe thirsty, and we have no water."

"Next time we get lost at sea, George," groaned Lorinda, "please don't mention water. I was fine till you said the word, and now I feel like I'm dying of thirst."

"Me, too," whispered Mildred. She passed her

tongue over her lips, and her eyes were large and frightened.

There was a long silence which they could actually feel pressing on their ears.

"I'm cold," said Mildred, her voice shaky.

"Shh!" warned George. "Listen!"

Far off to the left, they could hear the same low moaning sound they had heard the night before. It was like the cry of a feeble dying dog, but there was something human about it too.

"Oh my glory be!" gasped Lorinda.

"Yeah, I know," said George. "It's awful. But we'll have to take a chance. If it's from the land, like it was last night, we'd better follow it. If it's from somewhere else, well, we won't be much worse off than we were before. Unless it's got something to do with . . ." He stopped. "Let's go, Duncan!" he said. The moaning continued, and they followed it.

Mildred was sobbing quietly. "I'll never see Peterborough again," she choked.

"Yes you will, too," snapped Lorinda. "We're not in Spain yet. And shut up. We have to follow that moaning."

Mildred stopped crying, and all they could hear from her were swallowing noises.

Suddenly, through the fog, what looked like an immense wall appeared.

"My gosh!" exclaimed George, "We're just off

Black Head Cliffs. Lucky it's not blowing today, or we'd be as good as dead. But watch for those shallow rocks, Duncan. Say, guys, we sure drifted a long way."

"Look!" whispered Lorinda. "Look! Right over the stern!" And there, ghostly through the heavy mist, a boat of some kind was disappearing into the bank of fog. Suddenly it was gone, as though swallowed by the air. From behind the grey wall of fog, however, the moaning rose and fell like a cry of pain.

Now that they had found the shore, they followed it closely all the way back to Blue Harbour. In an hour they were tied up at the Government Wharf. Mrs. Dauphinee was standing there among the lobster pots in her apron, her face as white as paper. Jessie was hanging on to her hand.

"I told you!" she was saying fiercely. "You *promised*! How could you *do* this to me? I've been scared right out of my wits."

"Gee, Mom," said Lorinda. "I don't know what to say. I can't think of a good excuse. We all bent down to look at Mildred's fish, and then suddenly the land was gone. I didn't know it could disappear that fast."

"Well, it can! And after living in this place for eleven and a half years, it's time you knew that yourself!"

"I know, Mom," said Lorinda, as she climbed the ladder. "I'm real sorry. We always seem to be scaring you half to death." She put her arms around her mother and hugged her hard.

Mrs. Dauphinee hugged her back. "I'm so mad and so glad all at the same time," she said, her voice uneven. "C'mon home and get your dinner. Although it's probably all dried up by now. And Mildred . . ."

"Yes?"

"Your mother called. She'll call back this evening. I didn't tell her that her daughter was lost at sea." Mrs. Dauphinee was able to laugh a little. "And what's more," she went on, as they walked along the road towards home, "six strange men came down to the Harbour today. Not in uniforms or anything. They didn't talk to anyone. They just sort of walked around and, well, *looked*."

Lorinda put an arm around her mother and walked beside her. "Poor Mom," she said. "I guess it hasn't been your favourite day."

"No," grinned Mrs. Dauphinee. "It hasn't. But at least I see that we have a nice big fat mackerel for supper. Who's the big fisherman?"

"Me," said Mildred, smiling shyly.

Chapter 6
Halifax here we come

"There's a letter for you, Lorinda," said Mrs. Dauphinee, when they returned to the house. "I forgot to mention it on the Government Wharf. I was too busy thanking my lucky stars that you were all right, and wanting to string you all up by the thumbs for not being careful. I had no energy left in me to think about things like letters."

"Who from?"

"From that Jon man. Mr. Jackson. The man you claim to have rescued on the airplane trip to Toronto. His name's on the envelope."

Lorinda grabbed the envelope and ripped it open so fast that she tore the top of the letter. Laying it on the kitchen table, she smoothed out the torn part and started to read.

Dear Lorinda and James,

It seems a long time since I saw you, and I miss all of you a lot — you two and Hank and Sarah. And I won't be able to see you this summer because I'm doing a consulting job in Montreal until September.

Wait till you hear what happened to me last week. I was invited to give a talk to an organization in Toronto that helps people who have phobias. Like mine with airplanes. You can't believe how many things people are afraid of — bugs, closed spaces, open spaces, even *babies*. Can you believe it? I felt pretty proud of myself because all I was phobic about was airplanes, and besides, I'm a lot better. Mind you, when I went to Toronto to give the talk, I travelled by train!

And guess what I talked about? The trip I took to Toronto last January when I first met you. I told them how people with fears find assistance in the most unexpected places. And then of course I let them know how you helped me by being kind and patient, and even by being a little bit stern with me — the way Lorinda was when I refused to listen to your problems. The audience thought my talk was great, and they clapped and clapped.

I had thought I was giving the talk just to be helpful — a sort of charity. But just before I left, they handed me an envelope with a cheque inside. I feel that this money really belongs to you. I'll bet you'd like to do something special while the kids are visiting you.

Enclosed is the cheque they gave me. I've signed it over to you. I want you to go to the bank and cash it. Then take the money and use it to do something really exciting. You do the choosing. Someone once said to me that the best things in life are free in Nova Scotia, but I'm sure you can still find something to do with $100.

Your friend,

Jon

"*A hundred dollars!*" James' eyes were as big as frisbees as he peered over Lorinda's shoulder at the cheque.

Lorinda took the cheque and held it close to her chest. "I can't believe so much money!" she breathed. "Remember how much work it took to earn enough for that darn vase last Christmas? It would take us half the winter to make that much money."

"D'ya know what I think?" said Hank.

"No. What?"

"I think that when they open up the doors of heaven, Jon'll be the very first person they let in. All kinds of people will be waiting in line, and St. Peter'll yell out to them all, 'Go on back to the rear, you guys! This here man gets to come in before anyone else!' "

Mr. Dauphinee, mending nets by the fireplace, chuckled. "What're you gonna do with a fortune like that?" he asked. "Let me see, now. You could buy 200 fifty-cent ice cream cones. Or 100 lottery tickets. Or you could go to the barber and get twenty-five haircuts."

Lorinda was silent, frowning.

"Hey, Lorinda," said her dad. "What's the matter?"

"Nothing," she said. "I'm thinking. I'm just trying to forget your loony suggestions so I can think of a few that make sense."

"Halifax!" shouted James.

"What?" they all said.

"Halifax," he repeated. "Let's take the bus to Halifax on the first fine day . . ."

"If there ever is one," said Mildred.

James ignored her. "We'll go to Halifax and do a lot of cheap things and a bunch of expensive ones. Like we can feed breadcrumbs to the ducks in the Public Gardens. That's free, if Mom gives us the bread. We can climb up on the Citadel and show Mildred and Hank what an old fort looks like. That's free, too. We can go eat a meal in a restaurant and order anything we want. That's expensive. I saw Jon's bill after we ate in one of those fancy places in Toronto. It was a whole lot of money." James had tipped his chair back and was smiling and staring at the ceiling as though he were seeing a vision. "Then we can go down and watch the boats in the harbour. Free again. If we have money left over, we can buy things. I sure would like a new bell for my bike."

Mildred looked at Lorinda, eyes flickering with excitement. "Let's do that. Please, Lorinda."

Lorinda had never seen Mildred all lit up, and she couldn't pretend it wasn't happening. "O.K., guys," she announced. "The first fine day, we'll take the bus to Halifax and have ourselves a time!"

*   *   *

That evening, Mildred's mother phoned her. When the call was over, Lorinda asked her, "Well, how's your Mom? How's life in Peterborough?"

Mildred had a strange look on her face. "I don't know how anything is in Peterborough," she said. "They called from Long Island."

"From where?"

"Long Island. It's in the States. I guess the minute I was out of the house they hotfooted it for Long Island. For a month. Mom called to let me know where they were, in case I fell off a cliff or something I guess. Mom said they were having a heavenly time and that she wished I was there with them. Huh!"

"Whadda you mean, 'Huh!'," said Lorinda.

"I'm not going to try to explain."

A month! Well, thought Lorinda, we're sure stuck with her now. No matter how much she hates fish. No matter how many of us get leprosy.

*   *   *

The first fine day came two days later. When the big brown bus stopped at Jollimore's Corner, the four kids were ready to climb aboard. Mrs. Dauphinee was there to see them off, full of instructions. "Remember it's a big city. Watch the traffic lights. Don't accept any rides from anyone. Don't get lost or separated from each other. Don't miss the bus back home. And oh yes — have a good time!"

"Mom!" grinned Lorinda. "How can we have a good time if we're all tied up in knots with worry all the time? Keep your shirt on! We'll be fine."

Mrs. Dauphinee kissed all four of them, and they climbed on the bus. As it moved off towards Halifax, they could see her waving and waving on the edge of the road. "You'd think we were going off to war," sighed Lorinda.

"You're lucky," said Mildred. Lorinda stared at her. "My mom never seems to be around to do any worrying."

"Whaddaya mean? Not *around*?"

"Oh, I dunno. She's all the time going shopping for more clothes, or going to meetings and bridge games and cocktail parties and things. She doesn't seem to care what I do. She doesn't even *ask* me anything."

"Like what?" asked James.

"Like if I'm happy. Or who my friends are." She frowned. "Or if I have any," she added. "Like last night on the phone. She didn't ask if I was having a good time or anything. She just said, 'This is our phone number in Long Island in case there's an emergency.' Big deal!"

Lorinda didn't know what to say. So she didn't say anything. But every once in a while she sneaked a peek at Mildred, who was staring straight ahead looking forlorn.

"Hey, Mildred," Lorinda finally said, "you better look out the window instead of looking at the back of Hank's head all the time. You might see something."

"Like more Christmas trees," grumbled Mildred.

Lorinda sighed. Just when I think there's some hope for Mildred, she thought, she blows it. Every doggone time. Before long, however, she poked Hank and said, loud enough for Mildred to hear, "Keep watching. I know it all just looks like a forest, but in about a minute you're going to see a whole city just suddenly appear like magic beyond the trees."

And she was right. One minute they were in a wasteland of spruce and pine trees. Then they climbed a small hill, and there, stretching as far as they could see, was the city of Halifax — shopping centres, signs, traffic, noise. Large apartment buildings, and hundreds of small wooden houses coloured yellow, green, turquoise, white. The tower of Dalhousie University off in the distance. "Wow!" exclaimed Hank. "Sure is big!"

"Not as big as Toronto," said Lorinda, "but big." She knew she shouldn't say it again but she heard herself adding, "And lots bigger than Peterborough."

After they got off the bus, they headed for the Citadel, an old fort at the top of a high hill in the eastern part of town. They climbed all the way to the top of the hill and then stood on the edge of the moat which surrounded the fort. "A *real* moat?" asked Mildred, not believing.

"Yeah," said James. "Real. And plenty deep. But no water in it."

"They were ready to fight all kinds of battles to defend Halifax from this fort," explained Lorinda. "And look what we can see from here." They looked down over the centre of town, over the waterfront, at the tall buildings, at the ships coming and going in the huge harbour. And far off in the distance they could see the horizon and the open sea.

"Wow!" cried Mildred. "Wait'll I tell the Duke of York kids about *this*!"

"What?!" Lorinda could hardly believe her ears.

"Oh, nothing." Mildred looked down at her feet and kicked a pebble over the hill.

"Let's go in," said Lorinda, and they walked through the big gates into the centre of the Citadel, where soldiers in kilts were playing bagpipes and marching to and fro. Inside the fort, in the long stone rooms where soldiers had slept and eaten long ago, were several small museums. There were also stairways to lookouts and old gun stations.

"I never want to leave here," yelled Hank as he and James tore up and down the stone stairways. "Boy!" he chuckled when they stopped to peer down into the old moat. "Would your mum ever have a fit if she could see us standin' on the edge of this thing. One step and we'd be pushin' up daisies!"

When they came out of the fort, they ran down the side of the hill as fast as they could go. A short distance from the bottom, they threw themselves to the ground and rolled over and over. Then it was only a short walk to the Public Gardens where they fed the ducks, chased each other around the twisting pathways, looked at the flowers, sat on the benches in the shade and watched the swans on the pond.

"And all we've spent so far is the bus ticket," exclaimed Lorinda. "Let's buy a double-decker ice cream to keep us alive, and then go down Sackville Street to the waterfront." So they each bought a cone, and set off down the long steep hill to the harbour.

Down on Water Street were fancy stores, old stone buildings, giant wharves. In the distance they could see the two long bridges — graceful and strong, like iron birds — reaching across the water to Dartmouth. And there, tied up to a wharf, was the *Bluenose.*

Now, thought Lorinda. Now, at last, here's something to impress Mildred.

"May I introduce you two tourists," she said formally, bowing from the waist, "to the *Bluenose.*"

"The what?" said Hank.

"The *Bluenose.* Number II. Made exactly like the most famous vessel in the country!"

"In the *country,* my foot!" scoffed Mildred. "That little thing! I've seen lots bigger ships in Toronto harbour. There's one tied up to a wharf there, and anyone can go on it. And it doesn't have sails. That's *old* stuff. Ours is a *war*ship!"

"A *war*ship!" It was Lorinda's turn to be scornful. "Who the heck wants a *war*ship! The first

Bluenose was a peaceful ship. She was a schooner for catching fish. And she was a racer. She was in the big North Atlantic racing competitions long ago — with really important ships. And she won the Cup again and again — *five times*. Little old Nova Scotia beating the United States of America!"

Mildred was silent as they walked around the vessel, looking at her giant masts, the intricate network of ropes and ladders, the pulleys and lifeboats, the machinery.

"You shoulda seen her when the Tall Ships came," said Lorinda, her face eager with the memory of it.

"The what?"

"The Tall Ships. In 1984, huge sailing ships came to Canada from all over the world. The day they left Halifax Harbour, most of the other vessels went out under power."

"Under what?"

"With their motors on. Engines. Without many sails up."

"And?"

"And *Bluenose* sailed out with all her sails flying, leaning into the wind, and so beautiful we could hardly speak. We were that proud of her." Lorinda looked at Mildred. "She's on our dime, y'know."

"I don't believe it. That ship's just a big over-grown sailboat."

Lorinda dug in her jeans pocket and hauled out two dimes. "Heads or tails?" she said.

"Heads!"

"Tails!"

She flipped the coins. One came up heads and one tails.

"O.K. guys!" exclaimed Lorinda. "Look at the one that came up tails."

And there it was — *Bluenose*, sailing across the dime.

"Wow!" exclaimed Mildred, then turned and looked at the real ship.

"I got an idea," said James.

"What?"

"We were going to save most of our money for a big fancy meal and for presents for ourselves." They all nodded. "Let's get some fish and chips at that canteen over there" — he was pointing — "and then let's use our money to have a ride on the *Bluenose*. The sign says she leaves in twenty minutes, and it costs five dollars each."

"Sold!" yelled Lorinda.

"Holy jumpin's! Me for fish and chips and a boat ride!" That was Hank.

"And you, Mildred?" Lorinda spoke carefully.

"It's a lot of money. And I saw a really nice

store back there. And look at that super-duper restaurant down by the water. But . . . maybe if my mother knew I'd been for a ride on the boat that's on the dime, she might listen to me tell her about it." She paused. "Sure!" she said suddenly. "Let's go!"

Full of fish and chips, they bought their tickets and filed onto the vessel with the rest of the crowd. Before long, the anchor was raised, and *Bluenose* eased out from the pier. There was a strong offshore breeze. Before long her sails were set, and she was working out into the shipping lanes. Leaning into the wind, she moved like a huge silent knife through the water.

"Omigosh!" breathed Hank. "No wonder she won all those races!"

Mildred's eyes were bright as the boat sped past an oil rig, overtook a tugboat, swept by a container vessel moored to a wharf, slipped past George's Island and McNab's, and sailed into the open sea. Lorinda stood silent, her heart full, imagining she was a fisherman on the original *Bluenose* in days long ago, or the ship's captain steering her into port after an exciting race. She patted the side of the ship.

"Oh, *Bluenose*," she whispered. "I'm so proud of you!"

When the trip was over, they still had a piece of the day left before they had to catch the bus.

"Let's buy a present for your Mom and Dad," suggested Hank.

"Well . . ." said Mildred.

"Great idea!" said James.

And Lorinda announced, "I know exactly what they'd like."

"What?"

"A Nova Scotia flag for our flag pole. It hasn't had a flag on it since our last one was eaten up by a hurricane a few years ago. We forgot to take it down till it was too late. It just got chewed right up. They're on sale at that store over there for half price. I noticed a sign in the window."

"I did too," said James. "They're ten dollars each."

"Ten dollars!" exclaimed Mildred. "That's a lot of money!"

"*So?*" Lorinda's eyes bored into Mildred's.

Mildred looked at her and said nothing. Then — "So, fine," she said. "Let's buy one."

*   *   *

It was a long way to the bus stop. By the time they got there, their feet were sore and they were hungry again. Stopping at a lunch counter, they spent the last of their money on four hamburgers and about a bushel of chips. Then they climbed aboard the bus, sat down, and groaned — with tiredness, with relief, with satisfaction.

The last of the afterglow was colouring the sky as they travelled home along the shore road. The sea was glassy calm, as pink as the sky above it, and as they turned into the little road towards Blue Harbour, they saw a flight of gulls heading out to Pony Island and their nesting place.

"Ever pretty!" said Mildred.

Lorinda pretended not to hear, because she was afraid she'd say something like, "I told you so, dummy!"

Mr. and Mrs. Dauphinee were there to meet them at Jollimore's Corner, and they all talked at once, interrupting one another, almost yelling the news about their day. By the time they had walked the half kilometre to the Dauphinee's house, it was almost dark. They fell silent as they reached the veranda, turned, and stared out to sea.

And there were the lights. Flickering, winking, moving across the water. Mrs. Dauphinee shivered. "Come on inside," she said, "where it's warm." Then she added, "And safe."

Chapter 7
Digging for clams

"Another fine day!" Lorinda zipped up the blind and looked out the open window at the Harbour and the Bay beyond. The water was a deep rich blue, reflecting a cloudless sky, and she could tell just by looking at it — by *sniffing* it — that it was going to stay like that all day.

"C'mon, you guys!" she yelled. "When you get a day like this, you gotta *use* it. Let's get the Himmelmans and MacDermids and go dig clams on the Flats." Lorinda looked at Jessie's eager little face peeking out from under the blankets. "Aw gee, Jessie," she said. "I'm sorry. You can't come, because we have to go by boat. Mom says you can't go with us to the Flats until you're five. Two years to go." Jessie's eyes looked bleak now. Lorinda went over and picked her up, holding her on her lap for a few moments.

"Tell you what," she said, giving her a big squeeze. "I'll save eight of the very biggest clams

70

just for you. Then you can have your very own clam party when we get home."

"O.K.!" said Jessie, cheerful again. She hopped off Lorinda's lap. "I'm gonna play with Ivan." Ivan was the son of a couple who had moved into the Harbour a few months ago. He was four years old, and he and Jessie were already best friends. Jessie grinned at Lorinda. "Anyways, I don't want to spend a whole day with all you *old* people."

*   *   *

By 9:30, two dories set off from Mr. Coolen's wharf — one carrying Duncan and George and Fiona and Glynis, the other with Lorinda and Mildred and James and Hank. Duncan rowed the first dory, and Lorinda rowed the other. She was as big as the two older boys, and just as strong. They rowed around Pine Point and along the shore past Black Head Cliffs, avoiding the reefs. Almost a kilometre further along, there was an opening in the rocks, and they rowed into a sheltered cove that was shallow, with a broad beach of flat damp sand. Tying up their boats above the high tide line, they stepped out onto the beach. They took off their life jackets, hung them on a nearby tree, then unloaded picnic lunches, trowels, old spoons, buckets, and two black pots.

"O.K., you landlubbers," announced Lorinda,

"we'll show you how to do it. First you look for little holes in the sand."

"Pew!" sniffed Mildred. "What a *smell!*"

"It's an O.K. smell," said James. "All clam flats smell like this. I like it. It makes me know I'm home."

"It makes me know I'm *not*," declared Mildred.

"Well, stick it in the back of your head, and try to forget about it," ordered Lorinda. "See the holes? Those are for air. If you see a hole, you know there's a clam down there somewhere. Look!" She pointed to a hole and started digging in the sand with her bare hands. Soon she held up a big clam with its neck sticking out. The clam sucked it back in as soon as it hit the air.

"What on earth was *that?*" exclaimed Mildred, her face all screwed up.

"That was his neck," said Lorinda. "But he's tucked it into his shirt for now."

"*Yuck!*" Mildred almost spat the word out.

"Oh for Pete's sake, Mildred," growled Duncan. "It won't *hurt* you. It's only a *clam*."

"Get moving guys!" yelled George, who was handing out buckets. "Get to work. We can't eat them as long as they're all buried under the sand."

At first Mildred complained about the feel of the soft muddy sand. Then she worried out loud about her fingernails. After that she was afraid she'd cut herself on the shells. Everyone ignored her, although anyone close to Lorinda could have heard her muttering, "Shoulda brought along some goalie gloves for her. Or a muzzle. Or better still, left her behind to play with Jessie and Ivan." But as soon as Mildred found her first clam, everything was different. It's true that she dropped it like a hot potato when it stuck out its long neck, but it was a big clam and she was proud of it. They started to hear the clunk clunk of the clams as she dropped them into the bucket.

At 11:30, they all stopped for lunch, and lay around on the warm flat rocks to soak up some sun. All, that is, except Hank. He kept on digging like a crazed gopher. They fed him sandwiches as he worked, and his bucket — the biggest — was getting fuller and fuller. It wasn't until two o'clock that he stopped digging and threw himself down on the sand, above the line of seaweed left there by the last high tide.

"I'm gonna make a million dollars before I'm twenty," he breathed, "and build me a little house beside this place and live here forever. It's so beautiful I almost can't stand it."

"What about all the fog?" asked Mildred, wiping her wet hands on her pink pants.

"What fog?" asked Hank, grinning. "The Weatherman could give me two whole weeks of fog, and I'd forgive him if he sent me just one day like this one." He sighed, and then dropped off to sleep. Overhead there was a whispering sound in the spruce trees, and a single gull was coasting on the updrafts of wind. From afar, they could hear the waves breaking on the islands.

At four o'clock, the kids woke Hank up. They'd collected dry driftwood and some old logs, and had rigged up a big fireplace in the middle of a ring of granite rocks. Then they'd heated up a big pot of saltwater for the clams and a smaller pot of melting butter. By now, the clams were ready. Their shells had opened up, and the butter was hot and steamy.

"Get going, Hank!" cried James, poking him in the ribs. "If you thought *digging* clams was fun, wait'll you start *eating* them!"

Mildred was peering into the pot at the soft beige bodies of the clams in the open shells. "I never saw anything so disgusting in all my life!" she squealed. "You don't mean to tell me you're actually gonna *eat* those awful looking things? They look like lumps of putty — with tails. Ugh!"

Lorinda was about to tell Mildred what she thought about people who complained all the time, and who wouldn't even *try* anything. Then she looked at the piles of clams and thought, to heck with her. I've never in my whole entire life had enough clams to eat. I always want more when the

74

pot's empty. Maybe this is my big chance. Mildred can just sit on a rock and eat blueberries. Or starve. While we eat all her clams.

Lorinda called the others. They found a warm sandy spot and sat down in a circle. In the centre they put the drained clams and the pot of butter. Picking the clams up by their necks, they dipped them in the butter before popping them in their mouths.

Hank was like a wild animal. "Omigosh! Omigosh!" he muttered as he ate clam after clam. "Now I *know* I'm gonna come and live here. Maybe even before I get to be a millionaire. I could live here in a tent and have clams for breakfast, lunch and supper. Then I wouldn't have to bother ever going to heaven, because I'd be there already."

No one else said much of anything. They were too busy eating. But they did make happy grunting noises — umm, yum, wow, ohhh. Mildred watched from her rock, as she put blueberry after cold blueberry into her mouth. Finally she got up.

"I think I'd better just try one, so I can tell my dad I tried everything," she said, and joined the circle. No one paid any attention to her, except James who said, "Try closing your eyes when you eat them. Even Hank would tell you they aren't very pretty to look at."

"Oh no, he wouldn't!" mumbled Hank, between

clams. "He'd tell you that to him they even *look* gorgeous."

Mildred picked up a clam by its neck in her thumb and forefinger, dipped it into the community pot of butter, shut her eyes tight, and dropped it into her mouth. Then her eyes snapped open. "Oh!" she cried. "Oh my!"

"*Exactly!*" said Lorinda.

Now Mildred was eating fast to catch up. But with Hank's bucket still untouched, there would have been enough clams for a dozen people. When they'd eaten all they could, they stowed what was left in the boat to take to the three families back home. Lorinda put Jessie's eight giant clams safely away in a small pail.

"Better be getting home," she said, "before we scare Mom again."

So they threw sand on the fire and then water to drown it. They tossed the empty clam shells far out into the deep water, in case the fish wanted to eat any little bits that were left in them. They stuffed their other garbage in a plastic bag and put it in the boat. Hank collected all the shovels and spoons, and Duncan rounded up the buckets. Lorinda and Fiona scooped up the lunch leftovers and left them on a rock for the gulls, while George and James untied the boats. Glynis sat on a rock and looked at the view. "Thinking, as usual," growled George, "while we do all the work."

"Aw, leave her alone," said Lorinda. "She always helps when we need her, and someone has to do the thinking sometimes. At least she's always *cheerful*."

But even Mildred was looking pretty cheerful as they piled into the boats for their return journey.

* * *

The trip home was even calmer than the journey out, and they took their time. It was early evening as they came within sight of Blue Harbour. The sun was setting behind Mrs. Murphy's house, and the surface of the sea was like glass.

The sky had no red or pink in it at all, and clouds were starting to gather close to the horizon. Lorinda didn't say so, but she felt in her bones that bad weather was coming. Not just fog but wind maybe, and a lot of rain. Thank heavens, she thought as they entered the Harbour, that Dad does all his fishing close to land. That means we don't need to be chewing up our fingernails about him every time there's a storm. We don't have to worry about shipwrecks and drownings, or even about his old bronchitis anymore. It seems like that winter he spent in Texas fixed him up as right as rain. Instead of being sick half the time, he's almost as healthy as the rest of us now.

A few drops fell on Lorinda's head, interrupting her train of thought. Looking up, she saw clouds overhead that she hadn't noticed before. Tying up the boats at the wharf as quickly as they could, the kids grabbed their gear — oars, buckets, trowels, clams, sweaters, life jackets — and stumbled and ran for their homes. As Lorinda and Mildred and James and Hank tumbled through the Dauphinee's back door, the rain started to fall in earnest. It poured down so hard that even in the kitchen they could hear it pounding on the upstairs' roof.

"Wow!" panted James. "Listen to that! And we're not even wet. Are we ever lucky!" Then he saw his mother coming into the kitchen. "Hi, Mom!" he called. "We got a real big mess o' clams for you!"

They all started talking at once about the Flats, the clam bake, the perfect sunny day, the boat ride. Hank was shouting louder than anybody else. "I'm a Nova Scotian! I'm a Nova Scotian! Adopt me! Adopt me!" But James knew he didn't mean it. Hank loved his huge family, even though they had hardly any money and the adults were often out of work. James thought about all the fun he'd had in Peterborough with that big noisy bunch. Hank's shouting and even what he was saying were just ways of letting people know that he was happy. James could tell.

Just as he could tell that something was wrong with his mother, even though she was listening to their stories and smiling and asking questions. James had a smart way of knowing what was going on inside people's heads.

"What's wrong, Mom?" he asked.

"Nothing!" laughed Lorinda. "She's fine. She's cooking clams is what she's doing. Don't be such an old woman, James. She's fine!"

"She's not," said James. "Mom. What's the matter?"

Mrs. Dauphinee sighed and stopped smiling. "James is right," she said. "I'm worried, but it's probably silly of me. I guess it's because for so many years I had to fret about your father's health. After a while it gets to be a habit."

"And?"

"Well, he's gone off in the longliner for three days with the Jimson brothers. They couldn't find any crew, and they have to get the fish out of their nets before they rot. Everyone's gone to the Bridgewater Exhibition, so your father went out on the *Susie Elmira* with them. To save their fish, because they have so many mouths to feed. Nine kids between the two of them, not to mention their wives. I don't *blame* your father. I'm even proud of him. But it's so far to go. And now all this awful rain. I worry about his chest." She laughed in a shaky way. "Sorry, kids. I'm sure he's fine. I'm being stupid. It's just that he's so healthy now. I don't want anything to spoil it." Then she smiled — really smiled. "At least the Weatherman calls for good weather tomorrow."

Lorinda frowned. Well, *I* don't call for good weather tomorrow, she thought. The Weatherman is often wrong, but I'm almost always right. "And I can tell you right now," she whispered to Gretzky on the back porch, "there's going to be a great big storm. With wind and waves and rain. The works."

To her mother, Lorinda said, "He wants it fine for tomorrow? Great! Now get to bed early and have a good sleep." You're gonna need it, she thought.

Chapter 8
The big storm

Lorinda was right. When she and the others woke up the next morning, the sky was as dark as dusk, and the wind was so strong that there were white-caps even in the Harbour. Out on the Bay, the sea looked black and angry. From the kitchen window they could see the trees and bushes bending far over in the force of the wind. The radio was tuned to the Halifax station, and the weatherman was apologizing. "Sorry to have to report an unexpected low, arriving from the southwest up from the Gulf of Maine. We're now predicting gale force winds and heavy precipitation."

"What's 'cipitation?" asked Jessie.

"Rain," said James.

"Well, why don't they *say* rain, then?" whined Mildred.

"Because they don't." Lorinda looked at Mildred, at the storm, at her mother's troubled eyes. Something tells me, she mused to herself, that being nice to Mildred today is going to be rough going.

"Let's play Monopoly, eh, guys?" suggested James. He watched his mother out of the corner of his eye. "We've often had storms like this," he said, "and everything's always fine."

Not *always*, thought Lorinda. Two years ago, Mr. Piercey drowned off Black Head Cliffs in the tail end of a hurricane. She knew her mother was thinking about that, too. And the lights. How could you help but think about those lights when your father had been out at sea on a stormy night?

But Mrs. Dauphinee said, "It's O.K., kids. I called the Murphys. They said they picked up the Jimson boat on the ship-to-shore telephone, and everybody's fine."

"*Ship-to-shore!*" exclaimed Hank. "Ever neat! You mean you can talk to them from *here* when they're way out *there*?" He looked at the waves smashing against Pony Island and shivered.

"What did they say?" asked James.

"They said it was a big blow, but that the *Susie Elmira* was all right. They said the rain was something fierce." Mrs. Dauphinee sighed. "Go get the Monopoly set," she said. "It'll keep you all busy. Jessie 'n I'll make cookies."

Hank surprised everyone by winning the first two games. He looked so rough and tough that sometimes people forgot how smart he was. Mrs. Dauphinee looked over from the stove and chuckled,

"You'd better go into real estate when you grow up, Hank. You'd be rich in nothing flat."

"I'm sick of this old game," said Mildred, throwing down her money. "Isn't there *anything* else to do around here on a rainy day?"

Lorinda kept her cool. "C'mon, Mildred," she said, voice tight but even. "Just one more game. Let's try to make a poor man out of rich old Hank."

This time Mildred landed on Marvin Gardens, Ventnor Avenue and Atlantic Avenue within the first fifteen minutes. Then it was all downhill for the rest of them. No matter what else they bought, they kept landing on Mildred's property, with all its houses and hotels. When the game was over, Mildred sat there with piles of 500-dollar bills heaped up in front of her, all smiles.

"Mail time!" announced Mrs. Dauphinee. "You kids put on your rain gear and run down to the Post Office for me, will you? I'm expecting a letter from your Aunt Joan."

"You mean go out in *that*?" exclaimed Mildred. "We'll be soaked to our skins."

"Tough beans!" sniffed Lorinda. "Besides, I feel all logy and lumpy from sitting around so long. Anyway, when you're not too worried, a storm can be fun to watch and listen to. Wait'll you see the waves down by Pine Point."

They left Jessie at home — "She'd maybe blow

away," said James — and set off together. At the Post Office, they dripped their way across the floor to the counter.

"Ask if there's anything for me," whispered Mildred, and so Lorinda did. But there was nothing. "You'd think they could send me a postcard at least," sighed Mildred. Lorinda felt sad for her, thinking about all the letters she and James had got when they'd been in Peterborough. But she didn't feel sorry for long. Mildred complained all the way home.

"For gosh sakes, why does this road have to be so muddy? Why don't they pave it?"

And, "Jeepers, if they had a wind like this in Peterborough, the people would move out."

And, "No. I *don't* think the waves on Pine Point are beautiful. I think they're awful. It scares the daylights out of me just to look at them."

And, "For Pete's sake, when is that wind gonna *stop*? It's driving me *crazy*!"

And, "What on earth are we gonna do for the rest of the day? You haven't even got a colour TV. My jeans are soaked. I don't know why I ever came to this dumb province in the first place."

That did it. Lorinda stopped right in the middle of Blue Harbour's muddy road.

"Lookit, Mildred Walker," she started. "I don't know whatever made you come here in the first place, either. My beautiful province was getting along just great without you. You can stand there and get a whole lot wetter while I make you a little speech."

Lorinda stood facing into the wind, with her legs apart to brace herself, and glared at Mildred. The rain poured down their noses and drove against their raincoats and made sharp *clackity* sounds as it fell into the water lily pond near the road. There was something close to fear in Mildred's face. Lorinda's black eyes were needle sharp with anger, and she wasn't even aware of the wet or the cold.

"We've all tried really hard to be nice to you, Mildred. We're sorry your parents are never home and don't listen to you, but if all you do at home is complain, complain, complain, I wouldn't listen, either." Lorinda stopped long enough to take a deep breath and wipe the drip off the end of her nose.

Then she went on. "All you think about is you, you, you. You've never even *spoken* to Jessie since you got here. Don't you think she's a real live person — or *what*? She happens to be *nice*. I wouldn't even treat a dog like that. You hated Monopoly when you were losing, but loved it when you won. Once in a while you say something cheerful or nice, and before I can get used to the miracle, your mouth fills right up with meanness, and out comes a new complaint."

Lorinda thrust her head forward on her long thin neck, until her face was very close to Mildred's.

"Now you listen to me, Mildred. My dad happens to be out on that scary water in this wild wind. He has a weak chest, and he could get pneumonia. Or the boat could turn over and he could drown. What do you think of *that*? How do you suppose that makes my Mom feel? She's right crazy with worry, but what's she doing? She's making cookies and thinking up ways to keep us busy, so that we won't get too scared.

"*She's looking after us.* And we're looking after her, by pretending everything's fine, so she won't have to worry about us as well as about Dad."

Lorinda took a big gulp of the wet air and then went on. She was so mad she felt as though she could cut down twenty trees or row a boat to Spain — or yell at Mildred all day.

"So!" she continued. "Maybe you could just try to look after us, too. Like by shutting up about the mud and the wind and the black and white TV and your wet pants — and about every single solitary thing that you don't think is perfect. We're not in the mood for any of that junk today. Maybe you could even dream up something *nice* to say once in a while. My *gosh*!" Lorinda concluded. "You're almost as bad as Reginald Corkum!"

The four of them then walked home in silence.

For the rest of the day they read a lot of books and watched a lot of TV and played a lot of Scrabble and ate a lot of cookies. Lorinda got down on the floor and drew pictures with Jessie. Hank washed up Mrs. Dauphinee's baking dishes. James went out to the barn and talked to Petunia for a while. Petunia was their cow. "James always talks to Petunia when he's stirred up inside," explained Lorinda. "Me, I pick up Gretzky and hug him." She looked over at her mother, who was sitting by the window with her hands in her lap, rubbing her thumbs together. Then she looked over at Gretzky, who was sleeping, as usual, beside the wood stove. "C'mon, friend," said Lorinda, picking up the huge warm cat. "Someone needs you." Then she carried Gretzky over to her mother and placed him gently on her lap. Mrs. Dauphinee looked up and smiled. Then she stopped fiddling with her thumbs and started stroking Gretzky, softly, slowly. Gretzky narrowed his eyes and turned on his beautiful peaceful purr. "Thanks, Lorinda," said Mrs. Dauphinee.

Everyone went to bed early that night. The wind rattled the windows and howled in the hollow chimney. The sound of the water was loud on the pebbly beach in front of their house, and against the wharves and around the club poles. They all lay in bed and listened, until one by one they fell asleep. Out beyond Pony Island, the lights winked and shifted. They were the last thing Mrs. Dauphinee saw before she drifted off into a troubled sleep.

*   *   *

The next day was one of those fiercely beautiful Nova Scotia days, with the sky and sea a dazzling blue, and the whitecaps racing out to sea. The wind had changed, and was blowing strongly from the north.

"What do you think?" Mrs. Dauphinee asked Lorinda, as they stood by the window in their pajamas and looked out. Lorinda opened the front door and stepped onto the shaky veranda. She poked her head out beyond the railing and felt the wind. She sniffed the air. She looked up at the cloudless sky. Then she turned to her mother and grinned.

"Perfect!" she announced. "All day. By about three o'clock the wind'll die down and it'll start to warm up. A perfect kind of day for fishing — or for a return trip home. A perfect day for drying out wet clothes if you happen to be on a boat." She looked at her mother's troubled face. "Why don't you call the Murphys and see what the ship-to-shore telephone can tell us?"

"Well," Mrs. Dauphinee hesitated. "I'm dying to, but I thought it might be too early."

"With three kids under four years old?" Lorinda

laughed. "All the Murphys have probably been up since 5:30. Go ahead. Phone them."

Mrs. Dauphinee rose from her chair and went off to the hall to use the telephone. Lorinda went upstairs to put on her jeans and a warm sweater. When she came down, Mrs. Dauphinee was just standing in the hall, holding the receiver and staring into space.

"Mom!" Lorinda felt cold inside her warm sweater. "What is it?" Gently she took the receiver out of her hand and put it back on the hook.

"They've been trying since six o'clock to reach them. Susie Jimson called and asked them to." She paused. "Lorinda . . . "

"Yes?"

"They can't get any answer. There doesn't seem to be anything wrong with the phone, but nobody responds to their call."

Chapter 9
The long wait

It was almost noon now, and there was still no news from the *Susie Elmira*. Hank stood at the front door. The sun was high in the sky. "How come such bad things can happen on such a great day?" he muttered. Suddenly the offshore wind — the fine weather wind of Nova Scotia's South Shore — looked threatening to him. If the Jimson boat were adrift, it would be blown away from shore rather than back home. Of course no one knew where they were anyway, but drifting towards Europe or Africa was hardly what anyone hoped for. The Coast Guard had been called, and two of their men were out in the kitchen right then, getting information from Mrs. Dauphinee. Neighbors kept coming and going, asking questions, bringing brownies, offering to baby-sit in case Mrs. Dauphinee needed to go anywhere.

"Like where?" she asked. "The only place I want to go is out there" — she pointed out towards the horizon — "and even I know how stupid that would be." She sighed. "Thanks, but I want to stay right here. Near the phone. Where I can see the open sea." She hugged herself, then put another log on the kitchen fire. "I feel so cold," she added.

But now the Coast Guard officers were talking to her, and Mrs. Dauphinee was trying to explain to them exactly where the *Susie Elmira* had gone. She got out Mr. Dauphinee's charts and showed them where the fishing grounds were. Then she sent them over to the Jimson's in case they could learn anything more useful there.

Finally Mrs. Dauphinee rounded up the kids and told them to go out and try to enjoy the beautiful day. "Go on over to Elbow Beach and see what you can find in the way of beach treasures."

"Of what?" asked Mildred, who'd hardly spoken a word since yesterday.

"Beach treasures. Things that get thrown up on land in a storm. You nearly always find something, even if it's just a couple of pop bottles to return to the stores to cash in on." She smiled at them all. "Twenty-five cents to the person who finds the nicest treasure." She reached in her pocket and brought out a quarter. "No," she said. "Make it fifty cents," and she fished in her apron for another twenty-five cents. "We'll make it a big competition. Take Jessie. She could use a little fun, and she loves beachcombing. But *look after her*. I can only worry about one thing at a time right now."

A little while later they were on their way, each one carrying a green garbage bag. "Bring them back if you don't need them," called Mrs. Dauphinee from the back door. "Those things cost money. Besides, if you throw them in the sea, the bigger fish eat them and get sick."

It only took about ten minutes to get to Elbow Beach. When they arrived, they fanned out in different directions. Hank was the first to find something — a small blue plastic shovel. "For clams!" he yelled. Jessie picked up a sand dollar — a perfect one, with the star pattern dark on its light grey back. Mildred found a lobster trap. The net was in perfect condition and the little leather hinges on the door were unbroken. She nearly jumped out of her skin with excitement, until she realized that it was too big and heavy to take back to Peterborough on the plane. Then her face lit up. "I know!" she said. "I can give it to your dad as a coming-home present if he ever gets back. *When* he gets back, I mean." Lorinda's stomach shot right down into her feet, but she didn't say anything. After all, Mildred was trying. She just didn't know how to do it yet. "It takes practice," Lorinda said to Jessie.

Then Hank found a beautiful piece of twisted driftwood. "For your mom," he said. "To put a flower

pot in. I seen them like that often in store windows."
And James found a total of six beer bottles, worth
fifty cents in all, as he pointed out.

But it was Mildred who ended up finding the
best thing — a bright red and black lobster buoy,
hardly scratched up at all. "And small enough to fit
in my suitcase!" she announced. The only one who
didn't find anything was Lorinda. She didn't have
the heart to look very hard. She just trailed around
after Jessie and tried not to think. She watched the
little sandpipers skittering across the wet sand like
wind-up toys, before all rising together to fly in a
swarm over the water. She pointed out a shag — a
cormorant — to Jessie, and they laughed at the way
he stretched his long neck and flapped his huge
wings to dry them off. And today, with all that
wind, the gulls were having a ball, sailing on the
wind currents high above the beach. "So beautiful,"
Lorinda sighed, watching Jessie play tag with the
waves. "I wish I could enjoy it."

When everyone had done enough treasure-
hunting — when they had collected a metal door-
knob, a coil of yellow nylon rope, a rusty pie lifter, a
tiny glass bottle, a headless doll, and a jig frame —
they started for home. The wind had died down, just
as Lorinda had predicted, so they took off their
sweaters and dumped them into one of the garbage
bags. The sand was hot on their bare feet, and they

closed their eyes, putting their faces up to the sun to feel the warmth and the peace.

Then they heard the awful low moaning again. It seemed to be coming from behind an old shipwrecked dory. For a moment they stood as still as statues listening to the terrible sound. Then suddenly Hank dropped his garbage bag on the sand and raced over to the rowboat. Picking up sand, he threw handful after handful into the woods behind. Lorinda and James watched, fearful but unable to run. They remembered their father's warning about steering a wide berth around unknown dangers. And here was Hank heading right for the shoals. But when he finally threw a rock instead of sand, he got results. There was a yelp from behind the boat, and out jumped Reginald Corkum, howling, "Stop! Stop! You darn bullies!" Then he ran as fast as he could go down the shore path toward the village. As he slowed, they could see him walking along, shoulders slumped over, "looking" as James said, "as though he didn't have a friend in the world."

"Which he doesn't," snapped Lorinda.

"And doesn't deserve any," put in Mildred. "Of all the mean tricks! Scaring us half to death almost every day since I've been here." She put her fists on her hips and watched him skulk along home. "Some people make their so-called friends so miserable.

How can they enjoy spoiling everyone else's fun? Honest to Pete, it just makes me so mad!"

Lorinda gave Mildred a long, hard look, but didn't say anything. She figured she'd said enough the day before. But Mildred's eyes shifted away, and she picked up her garbage bag and started for home.

"Well," sighed Lorinda to James. "I wish all our other mysteries and worries could end up with an answer as simple as that one. I almost feel grateful to old Reginald for taking my mind off things that are more important than he is."

* * *

At the Dauphinee house, the kitchen seemed to be full of strangers. There were two Mounties drinking coffee and eating Mrs. Dauphinee's cookies. There were three neighbors standing in a line, each holding what looked like a hot casserole. And there was a reporter and a photographer from *The Mail-Star* standing at the door. They seemed to be hounding Mrs. Dauphinee with questions, and she looked frantic enough, as Lorinda said later, to self-destruct into smoke any minute.

"I've told you everything I know," she was saying in a shaky voice. "Why don't you go over to the Jimsons and pester them instead?"

"Just one minute, Mrs. Dauphinee," interrupted the photographer. "Are all those little kids with the green garbage bags your children?"

"Well, yes. I mean no," she said. "Some are. Three of them. The others aren't."

"I think I'll just get a picture of those poor little children," he said. "Maybe grouped around the table with you in the middle? We're always looking for human interest, and this sure fills the bill."

Lorinda was ashamed of how fast she moved toward that table. As she rushed forward to get her picture taken, worry was still making a big empty hole in the centre of her stomach. But she was thinking excitedly, I'm gonna have my picture in the newspaper. I'm gonna be splashed all over *The Mail-Star*. And she was liking that. What kind of a person am I, anyway, she wondered, to be thinking things like this when my dad is maybe on the bottom of the ocean? In the picture — when it appeared in the paper next day — she was clutching her big green garbage bag and smiling, but her eyes were sad. She cut out the picture and pasted it in her scrap book. But she never really liked it.

That evening they had one of the casseroles for supper, and brownies for dessert. During the meal, Mrs. Dauphinee presented Mildred with her fifty cents for finding the best treasure on the beach. Then Mildred and Hank did the dishes while James and Lorinda took turns answering the telephone.

Mrs. Dauphinee gave Jessie a bath and read her a story. The older kids were careful to look cheerful and to pretend they weren't worried. But they might as well have saved their energy. It seemed like every few minutes Jessie asked, "Where's Daddy? Where *is* Daddy?" And Mrs. Dauphinee had to keep saying, "Out there somewhere. Maybe he'll come home tomorrow."

* * *

That night before bedtime they all went to the window to look out at the lights. And found themselves staring at something even more frightening. Darkness. Total darkness. Even though it was clouded over, a perfect night for the lights to be putting on a show, they weren't there. Where had they gone?

"What does it mean?" whispered Hank.

But no one had an answer.

Chapter 10
Danger on the beach

The next day, everyone woke up early. Though they hadn't slept much — Mrs. Dauphinee almost not at all — they were wakened by their fears. They all got up and dressed quietly, their faces serious and careful. Only Jessie was in high spirits, although Mildred had a peaceful look — sober but contented — as she bustled around being useful. "The child is blooming," commented Mrs. Dauphinee, watching her as she accepted yet another tin of brownies from a neighbour. When the neighbour said, "How lucky the Dauphinees are to have you here to help!" Mildred turned a hot bright pink, and smiled all the way to the refrigerator. When Jessie asked, for the tenth time that morning, "Where's Daddy?" Mildred took her by the hand and led her upstairs, where she read her five stories, one after the other.

"Seeing is believing, I guess," commented Lorinda.

Outdoors, warmth shone down on the little village and the Bay was sparkling with reflected light.

By nine o'clock, men were returning with the morning's catch, trailing strings of boats behind them. Hank and James stood on the veranda and watched it all. Hank kept sighing, "Only two more weeks, and it'll all be over." Then he looked at James' sad face, and said, "Gosh, James, I'm sorry to act happy when you're feeling so terrible. I just can't help it. I guess I'm a bad person."

"Don't be dumb," said James. "It helps us a lot that you go around looking so cheerful. Some of it even rubs off on us. Enjoy yourself. He's not *your* father."

"Just what I was about to say," said Mrs. Dauphinee, joining them on the veranda. "About enjoying yourselves, that is. No point in staying around here and glumphing. Don't waste this perfect day. Get out there and make use of it."

"Well . . ." hesitated James.

"Look," she said, "I really need to keep busy. I'd like to put a pile of Indian Pears in the freezer for next winter. But I can't do it if I don't have any. So you could get the berries for me. I'll drive the four of you out to the Hidden Cove road. It's about three more kilometres from there to the Berry Grounds, but the walk will do you good. It'll tire you out and make you sleep tonight. And it's lovely there — all those giant rocks and bluffs and places to sit and hide and just *be*. Always before, we've gone as a special treat. This time you can just go, all by your-selves. The view there is the best along the shore, and the little sheltered beach is so safe and quiet."

Hank looked so lit up about it that James said, "O.K. Mom. A good idea." Then Jessie began to plead from the doorway. "Please, please, please, *please*, Mummy. Can I go too?"

"Oh Jessie!" Mrs. Dauphinee's eyes were trou-bled, and she sighed. "I hate always to be saying no, but it's so far, and a little bit dangerous — on the big rocks and all."

"Mrs. Dauphinee," Mildred interrupted from behind Jessie, "I promise I won't let her out of my sight for two seconds. There are four of us, too. We can take turns carrying her if she gets tired, and we can tie her to a tree while we're picking the berries."

"Aw, Mom!" This time it was Lorinda speaking. "Let her come. We sometimes do dumb things, but one thing we're always careful about is Jessie."

Mrs. Dauphinee thought for a few moments. "Well," she said slowly, "It's against my better judg-ment, but yes, you can take her. I've said no to her so many times this week that I just can't do it again this morning."

So they all dashed around getting ready. Mrs. Dauphinee packed a quick lunch that would be light to carry, and she added a length of rope for tying Jessie to a tree. "And a reef knot, mind!" she warned

Lorinda. "A good tight one." By ten o'clock they had all piled into the truck and were heading down the road to the turnoff for Hidden Cove.

At the crossroads, the kids jumped out of the truck and waved goodbye to their mother. "Sure you're O.K., Mom?" asked James.

"Sure," she said. "Fine. Aunt Joan's coming out from Halifax to be with me, and we'll have a good old time." She started the car and leaned out the window.

"Remember, now," she yelled to them. "Be *careful*. And glue yourselves to Jessie." As she drove off, she sighed. "Oh dear," she said out loud to herself, "I hope I was right to let them go."

When she reached home, Aunt Joan was waiting. She'd brought along — guess what? — another tin of brownies and a large casserole.

* * *

The road to Hidden Cove was beautiful. Though wide enough for a car, it was seldom used, and the surface was soft and grassy, with wildflowers along the edges. There were August flowers, and butter and eggs, and daisies, blueberries of all kinds and foxberries, too. But they didn't stop. "Wait'll you see the Indian Pear bushes," said Lorinda. "Picking Indian Pears is easier than falling off a tree. You don't even have to bend over."

No one had to carry Jessie even once on the way in. She seemed overloaded with energy, and was so excited about being with them that she never even mentioned being tired. Halfway down the road, they passed a small truck. "I hope no one got to the trees before us," said James. But when they arrived, the tall bushes were fuller than they'd ever seen them, and there was no one in sight.

Before doing anything else, they threw themselves down on the warm ground and rested for a while. Then they tied Jessie to one of the Indian Pear trees and set to work. At first, they ate everything they picked. The Indian Pears were bigger than blueberries and ripe and purple; and everyone was hungry. "We'll do the heavy picking after lunch," said Lorinda.

From the group of trees, they could see the huge stark rock bluffs at the end of the grassy road, and beyond them the edge of the little beach at Hidden Cove. "That's where we'll eat our lunch," said Lorinda. She didn't notice that Hank was exploring the territory or that he was climbing a nearby hill. Suddenly he was back beside her.

"Lorinda!" he whispered, and beckoned to the other kids to gather round. "There's all kinds of people down there on the beach. And between the rocks on the bluff. It don't look right to me. Lorinda — c'mon up and look. The resta you stay here. And don't make no noise. I don't wanna go back to Peterborough with a bullet in my head."

"Bullet!" Mildred's eyes looked stuck open.

Lorinda and Hank were halfway up the hill already. At the top, Hank motioned her to squat down. "Your red shirt will look like a flag up here," he warned.

Lorinda looked down and gasped. There were five men on the beach packing stuff into fish boxes. Nearby, two others stood, holding what certainly looked like guns. A small motorboat was anchored offshore, and a little flat was drawn up on the sand. Further up the beach, above the high tide line, was a larger flat, tied to a rock.

"I don't understand," whispered Lorinda. "No one ever fishes here. It's not a place where fish come. Not ever. And those can't be guns, but they sure look like them."

Then Hank pointed the other way. "I can't see too good," he said. "The teacher says I need glasses. But maybe you can see what's goin' on between them two giant rocks." Lorinda looked over to the bluff where he was pointing. She had to stuff her fist in her mouth to keep from screaming.

"Hank!" She grabbed his arm when she dared take her hand away from her mouth, and spoke in a hoarse whisper. "That's Dad and the Jimsons down there! They're tied up. And that man beside them

. . . he really does have a gun. I can see it." Pulling Hank behind her, she turned and ran down the other side of the hill.

By the time they reached the others, Lorinda had calmed down, and was icy cool and strong.

"Listen, kids," she said in a loud whisper. "We gotta get out of here, and fast. Don't say *one word!*"

"I'm tired!" said Jessie, her voice like a bell. "I wish . . . " But Lorinda had clapped her hand over her sister's mouth.

"I'm sorry, Jessie," she whispered, "but listen hard. Daddy's down here. Tied up. And there are men with guns. So it doesn't matter if you're tired. And if they hear us, we could be tied up too. Or worse. So — *no one can talk*. Get your gear, and get moving. *All* your gear. It's gotta look like we were never here."

Never did five kids move more quickly or more silently. Within five minutes they were on their way back down the Hidden Cove road. It was tough going. They were tired, hungry and scared, and they had to take turns carrying Jessie. They also had to move as fast as they could. They figured that the boxes those men were packing were going to end up in the truck they'd seen. When that happened, the truck would start moving. And it could go a lot faster than they could.

"There it is!" whispered James, as they passed

the pickup truck. He suddenly turned around and raced back, opened the door and peered in. Then he disappeared into the cab and came out again. He was waving something in his hands.

"The keys!" breathed Lorinda. Good old James, she thought to herself. So quiet that some people think he's dumb. Smartest dumb person I ever met!

Then Hank ran back to the truck too. Kneeling down, he fiddled with one of the tire valves. Even from where the others stood, they could hear the hissing sound.

"Now we really do have to hurry," said Lorinda when James and Hank caught up with them. "If they reach that truck they'll know someone has been fooling around with it. And they'll be *mad*. So let's get moving!" They stumbled along as fast as they could, panting and groaning. Every so often Lorinda would stop and say, "Listen! Can you hear anything? We have to be ready to dive in the bushes if they get near us." But each time, all they could hear were their own racing heartbeats.

It seemed like forever before they reached the end of the Hidden Cove road, but they finally arrived at the main highway.

"Oh my gosh!" gasped Mildred. "I forgot that it's still three kilometres to home from here! Oh my gosh!" Then she stopped short. "I'm not complaining," she said. "Just mentioning it."

Lorinda gave a little nervous laugh. "Your complaining is the least of my worries right now, Mildred. But never mind. You're doing O.K. And don't worry. This is a busy road. We're not going to have to walk very far."

As she spoke, a small truck approached from the direction of Blue Harbour. Lorinda stood in the middle of the road and waved her arms around. The truck stopped, and the driver leaned out the window. "Gotta problem?" he asked in a lazy voice.

"You wanna believe it!" breathed Lorinda. "Please. It's a terrible emergency. Can you take us to Blue Harbour?"

"Sorry, kiddo," he drawled, "but I'm going in the other direction. As you can plainly see. Now, get outta the road and let me pass!"

Lorinda's legs felt like tree stumps and her arms ached from carrying Jessie.

"My *father's* out there!" she pointed to the Hidden Cove road, pleading. "In danger. Tied up. Someone may kill him if we don't hurry!"

"Oh sure!" sneered the man. "And I'm Michael Jackson." He ground his gears into position and took off down the road.

The small parade of tired kids continued their journey, and before too long another truck stopped. This time, although the man obviously didn't believe Lorinda's story, he said, "Sure. Pile in the back, kids. Blue Harbour's on my way. It's a pretty crazy story to tell to get a drive, but I'll take you anyway."

"Oh, thank you, mister!" said Lorinda. Then, noticing that the truck was moving slowly, she yelled out to the driver, "Can't you go any *faster*?" When the man frowned, she added quickly, "My little sister needs to go to the washroom, and she's sitting on top of your fish." The man revved up his engine, and his truck raced down the road.

When they reached Blue Harbour, Lorinda pointed out their house. As they drew nearer, the truckdriver's eyes widened. Around the little house were a Coast Guard truck, two RCMP officers, a reporter, a photographer, and a small army of village women.

"See?" said Lorinda to him as she got out of the truck. "You'll probably end up on the front page of *The Mail-Star*. For rescuing the poor Dauphinee children from certain death. Thanks, mister. Now, I gotta go."

It didn't take James and Lorinda long to tell their story. The RCMP and the Coast Guard officers talked together and made a few phone calls from behind the closed doors of the front hall. "We may need a helicopter," a Mountie explained to Mrs. Dauphinee, "but we're going to try a surprise manoeuvre first. That man of yours is in big danger, and we have to move real slow. Our first plan is to get to that truck before they do. And we'll have a boat standing by to pick up the survivors, if that works." He rubbed his hands together. "It's all coming together, now. Thanks, kids. You've probably saved three men — and something else I can't tell you about yet."

Mrs. Dauphinee didn't like the sound of that word "survivors." Or "probably." What about anyone who *didn't* survive? What about those guns?

"Please!" she called out to them as they headed for their cars and boats. "Be *careful!*"

*   *   *

In the meantime, the truck driver was posing beside his truck with a big smile on his face. The photographer took twelve pictures of him.

Chapter 11
A mystery solved!

"This is the longest afternoon of my whole life," sighed Hank, and he spoke for all of them. Mrs. Dauphinee just paced around, twisting her apron. She even forgot to remind them to eat their picnic lunch, until at three o'clock Jessie said, "Aren't we gonna eat, *ever*?" and Lorinda went and opened their lunches. Four or five village women had come to call, but none of them knew what to say or do, so they just sat around in the kitchen and said nothing. All you could hear was the slow ticking of the kitchen clock and the sound of kids chewing. At last the phone rang. Mrs. Dauphinee flew out to the hall to answer it, but when she got there she pressed her hand over her heart and looked afraid to pick it up. "Please, please," she whispered, her eyes closed. Then she lifted up the receiver and said, very softly, "Hello?"

The man on the other end was so excited and talked so loudly that she had to hold the phone away from her ear. This meant that the kids, crowding around her, could hear every word that was said.

"This is Lieutenant O'Malley," the man on the other end yelled, "calling from Lobster Point. Can you hear me? I can hardly make you out."

"Yes," replied Mrs. Dauphinee. "Go on. Hurry."

"It was a drug run," he shouted. "One of the biggest ever on the East Coast. Dozens of kilos of cocaine and heroin. Bound for New England and Toronto. Worth over two million dollars."

"Never mind the money," pleaded Mrs. Dauphinee. "Is my husband O.K.? Is he safe?"

"This is how we did it, ma'am," he said. "We waited beside the truck till they came, and then we jumped them. A perfect manoeuvre. We didn't have to fire a shot. Caught red-handed with all the hot stuff right on them. Oh, Mother McCree!"

"My *husband!*" Mrs. Dauphinee's voice was rising.

"Oh, yes," said the Lieutenant. "Him. Well, it took a while."

"So I notice," she retorted.

"First of all we had to tie them up. At the truck, I mean. Handcuff them and all. Can't do that in five minutes, y'know."

"*Is my husband all right?*" Mrs. Dauphinee was actually yelling into the phone.

"Well, Mrs. Dauphinee," he began again. "It

was like this. You know those lights that you all been watching? Well, they were pretty smart. The men, not the lights. They rigged up that fancy system with real boats and sometimes real men, and sometimes tape recorders. We went out from time to time to ask them questions, but we never could pin anything on them. And their answers sounded so fishy that we thought they had to be up to something really big. So after a while we stopped bothering them and just set up observers to keep an eye on them — hoping to trap them. Then, while the whole shore and half the Coast Guard and RCMP in the area kept their eyes on what was going on out *there*, they upped and did all their serious business farther down the coast."

"Lieutenant!" cried Mrs. Dauphinee. *"Please!"*

"Oh, rightie-O!" he replied. "You maybe want to know what we did after the men were stashed away in our patrol car."

"No!" she snapped. "I just want . . ."

"Well," he went on, "two of our best men — trained in guerrilla work, y'know — went back to the bluff and moved around behind the rocks. A perfect place for an ambush!" he exclaimed. "Lots o'places to hide, and you can walk around as silent as a cat. There was only one man guarding them, but he sure had one deadly gun in his hands."

"Oh my sweet heavenly days!" groaned Mrs.

Dauphinee, and sat down on the bottom step of the front stairs, holding her forehead. "Can't you just tell me . . . "

Suddenly Lorinda grabbed the phone. "Listen Lieutenant Whoever-you-are," she shouted, "you've been sitting around our kitchen for two days, eating my mother's cookies and drinking nineteen million cups of expensive coffee, and making like you were our boarders, and enjoying all those chicken casseroles and brownies." She paused for a moment for breath and to decide whether or not she should say what came next."While five two-bit kids went over to the Berry Grounds and solved your case for you." She'd made her decision. Her voice rose. "You tell my mother *yes* or *no* if our father is alive and O.K., or else I'm gonna let the air out of all the tires in the cars and vans that you've left sitting in front of Petunia's barn!"

There was a very slight pause at the end of the line. Then "Yes," came the voice, much quieter now. "He's fine. He's O.K. So are the other men. One of our officers fired a shot in the air from behind a rock. Then when their guard turned around to shoot back, our other man jumped down on him from a rock ledge and pinned him to the ground. It was all over in less than two minutes." Then they could almost hear him grinning through the phone. "If I don't get a promotion for this, I'll eat my brass buttons!" Then he added, "You're not the only ones who solved this case, young lady!"

Lorinda wasn't finished speaking. "O.K. And thanks. But where are they *now*? When'll they be *home*? How are you *getting* them here?"

"Well," began the Lieutenant, "It's like this. After we . . . "

Lorinda interrupted him. "Did you hear me, Mr. Lieutenant? My father has a weak chest, and right now my mother is nearly crazy with worry. Not to mention us or the neighbours who are standing around with more pans of brownies. Where *are* they? When will they be *home*?"

"They're almost on their way," he replied at last. "Our men are taking them by boat. And towing their flat. They should be arriving in about fifteen minutes. Listen, don't you want to hear how it all happened? In the big storm, your father and his pals piled into their big rowboat when their longliner's engine failed and the vessel sprang a leak and started drifting towards the east. They rowed for nine hours until they finally came ashore in the dark, at the very spot where these six men were about to make millionaires of themselves."

But the Lieutenant might as well have saved his breath. There was nobody left to listen to him. They were all on their way to the Government Wharf, racing as fast as their legs could carry them.

In a village the size of Blue Harbour (twenty houses, seventy-three people and a lot of party lines), news travels fast. By the time they reached the Wharf, there was a crowd on it. Everyone seemed to know about the drug bust and that Mr. Dauphinee and the Jimsons were safe.

"If there's seventy-three people who live in Blue Harbour," said Hank. "I betcha there must be seventy here right now. Not countin' me and Mildred. Boy! Some big crowd!" The Himmelman kids were there, of course, and the MacDermids. Mr. Himmelman had even stayed home from work in Halifax because of his fears for Mr. Dauphinee and the Jimsons.

Suddenly there was a little silence, and through it came a voice — a *kid's* voice — loud and clear:

"How come Mr. Dauphinee was there right when the drugs came in? Seems kinda fishy to me!"

"Reginald Corkum!" whispered Lorinda. She dug her fingernails into her palms and listened.

"Missing from home for two whole days, and then look where he turns up! Right in the middle of a gang of drug traffickers."

The silence on the wharf was terrible. No one liked what Reginald was saying, but no one could stop listening, either.

"And everyone knows," he went on, "how much

that family needs money. Boy, if I was them Mounties, I'd sure ask a lot of questions!"

Suddenly Lorinda saw Mildred break away from their group, just as the Coast Guard boat could be seen rounding Rocky Point. She walked right up to Reginald and glared straight into his eyes.

"You two-bit nerd!" Mildred hissed. "You dried up piece of flesh! You twerp with the big fat ugly mouth! You and everyone else on this wharf knows that Mr. Dauphinee is the nicest darn father in Blue Harbour. Maybe," and here her voice trailed off a bit, "the nicest one in the *world*." Then her voice got strong and fierce again. "That guy is so sweet and honest that he wouldn't keep a ten cent piece that didn't belong to him. In on the drug bust! What a laugh! That's such an awful idea that I'd kill you dead as a squashed toad if I didn't find it so funny!" Then she threw back her head and roared with laughter. And right along with her, the whole wharf-full of people burst out laughing, and then cheered and clapped.

Lorinda stared at Mildred, and could feel tears in her eyes. Mrs. Dauphinee, laughing and crying all at once, went over and folded Mildred in her arms.

By then the boat was so close to shore that they could see Mr. Dauphinee and the two Jimson men wrapped in blankets, grinning all over their faces and waving. Then another cheer went up, and before long the boat was tied up to the wharf. In less than a minute, the men had climbed up the ladders and were hugging their families and shaking hands with the other men.

After this came questions, questions, questions, and the photographer from *The Mail-Star* took so many pictures that it's a wonder he didn't run out of film. He kept muttering, "Human interest! Oh, wow!"

It was at this point that Mrs. Dauphinee stepped forward and broke it all up.

"You've got the rest of the year to ask all those questions," she announced. "And to answer them, for that matter. My husband," and here she beamed at Mr. Dauphinee under his red blanket, "has bad lungs. And he's been outside two days in wet weather and wind. You can just put that camera of yours away. You must have enough pictures by now to fill six newspapers. I'm tired of being a famous family, and I'm taking my man home so I can feed him chicken casserole and brownies and put him to bed with a hot water bottle."

It was such a long speech for Mrs. Dauphinee, that when she was finished everyone clapped, just as though it had been some kind of dramatic performance. She smiled shyly at them all, and then she took Mr. Dauphinee's arm and set off for home.

*   *   *

Right after supper, James ran a hot bath for Mr. Dauphinee. Lorinda dumped a whole pile of "Flowers of Acadia" bubble bath into it — a gift from Aunt Joan the previous Christmas. Hank helped by putting three hot water bottles in Mr. Dauphinee's bed, along with an extra comforter from his own bed. Mildred brought a jar of daisies in and put them on the bureau. When Mr. Dauphinee finally got under the covers, he said he felt like a king in a royal palace. He looked tired, but he looked fine, and no matter how hard Mrs. Dauphinee listened for it, there wasn't a sign of a cough. Then all the kids took turns tucking him in, and plumping up his pillows, and asking him questions. But when they got to the fourth question, there was no answer. They looked at him, and he was fast asleep — still sitting up, with the light shining right in his face, and with Gretzky and Jessie both sitting on top of him.

"Tired!" said Hank.

*   *   *

After she said good night to all the kids, Mrs. Dauphinee walked out onto the veranda in her dressing gown and stood there for quite a long time, looking far out to sea. She listened to the "mmmmm*uh*" of the Groaner buoy and to the water as it swirled around the spiles on the wharves. She thought about the night before when she'd been angry at the sea, finding all its sounds and smells unfriendly and sinister. She sighed a peaceful sigh, and as she looked out over the open water and the darkening sky, she smiled.

"Thank you," she said, right out loud.

Chapter 12
Goodbye, goodbye

The next two weeks flew by. Everyone was surprised when suddenly there was only one day left
before Mildred and Hank had to go home. By then,
they had become part of the Blue Harbour family —
Lorinda and James and Jessie, Duncan and Fiona,
George and Glynis, Hank and Mildred. Hank was
used to having lots of people around, so he was com-
fortable with all the noise and arguments and
laughter. But Mildred, an only child who had
always dreamed of being part of a big family, didn't
know exactly how to handle it. She was happy, but
in a kind of silent wide-eyed way. Arguments scared
her. Was her beautiful new family going to fall
apart? When she discovered that their closeness
could survive squabbles and different ways of
looking at things, she was almost afraid to believe
it. When everything was going well — which was
most of the time — she kept worrying about how
long it would last.

Reginald was the only one outside this village

group. Even Ivan, the little new boy, had found his place already. It seemed that every time anyone even thought of inviting Reginald along, he'd do something terrible just before the invitation was delivered. James kept saying that he might be nice to *them* if they'd be nice to *him*, but after the scene on the wharf two weeks ago, Lorinda wouldn't even discuss the matter. All she said was, "It'd be like being friendly with a man-eating shark. No *thanks!*"

That night, the night before Hank and Mildred were to catch the 8:40 a.m. flight to Toronto, the Himmelman and MacDermid kids came over to say goodbye. Hank was so silent that no one knew how to treat him. Mildred spent most of the evening crying. Finally, Mr. Dauphinee took all the children down to the beach to skip stones in the moonlight. This just made Mildred cry all the harder. Hank said, "I know it's the same old moon as we got back home, but somehow it don't look the same." Finally, Mr. Dauphinee said to the Harbour kids, "How be you all come to the airport with us tomorrow morning? There's lots of room in the back of the truck for the Himmelmans and MacDermids."

The next day, the Dauphinee kids helped cart out the luggage from the house. Mildred was wearing the same hot pink pants and frilly white blouse she had arrived in. Mrs. Dauphinee had washed and pressed them for her the day before. Hank looked like he always did — as though he'd slept in his clothes and lost his comb a week ago. When Mr. Dauphinee suggested that Lorinda and Mildred sit up front, Mildred pleaded with him: "Aw please, Mr. Dauphinee. Never mind my pink pants. It's more fun in the back with the others. Besides, if Lorinda and I go back there, maybe Mrs. Dauphinee and Jessie could come, too. They could go up front and keep you company."

In the end, the whole family came. All the older kids — Lorinda and James and Duncan and Fiona and Glynis and George and Mildred and Hank — sat on cushions in the back, bundled up in blankets against the chill of the early foggy morning. "Arrive in a fog, leave in a fog," grinned Mildred. "But it sure looks different to me than it did four weeks ago." They could see the outlines of the fish stores and the trees just beginning to appear on the other side of the Harbour, and the fog was turning a bright glowing yellow to the east of their house.

"Gonna be a fine day," said Lorinda. "I can feel it."

Just then the old familiar moaning came from a clump of bushes close by. Hank slid out of the back of the truck and tiptoed over. Taking a whistle out of his pants pocket, he blew it as hard as he could, right into the middle of the bushes. Out leapt Reginald Corkum, hands clapped over his ears. Everybody laughed.

Then Hank sobered up and said, "Hey, guy. Don't have a fit or nothin'. We ain't mad at ya."

"Oh aren't we, though!" growled Lorinda, through clenched teeth.

But Hank went on. "You just made our adventures more exciting. Boy, will I ever have big wild tales to tell back in Peterborough. I bet nobody'll believe them. I'll make that moaning of yours sound like just about the scariest thing in the world." Hank moaned, trying to imitate Reginald, and then laughed again.

Reginald just stood there. One solitary tear shivered at the bottom of his eye before rolling slowly down his cheek. Before he could wipe it away, everyone had seen it.

"Why's he crying?" whispered Lorinda, puzzled.

"Maybe James is right," said Mildred. "Maybe he wants to be nice, and just doesn't know how to do it." She paused, and looked down at her feet. "Some people are like that, y'know," she mumbled.

Then suddenly James spoke. He didn't ask Lorinda or even his parents. He yelled, "C'mon, Reginald! There's lots o' room in the back o' the truck. Jump in. It's time you saw an airport!" To Lorinda he whispered, "Calm down. If you think

he'll pollute the truck, you can wash it down afterwards."

Reginald paused for a moment, not speaking.
Then he rushed forward and scrambled on board.
On the way to the airport, he didn't say one single
word. He didn't laugh or talk or join in the fun or
yell when they went over bumps. He didn't even
smile. But his eyes were shining, and his hands
were clasped together so tight that the knuckles
were white.

*   *   *

On the way back from the airport, everyone was
quiet — thinking, remembering, missing the visi-
tors already. Mrs. Dauphinee and Jessie rode in the
back to give Jessie a treat, but even she was silent.
The sun had burned through the fog, and the Bay
was dazzling as they turned down onto the shore
road. The wind had come up, and the offshore reefs
were alive with white breakers blowing into the
sky. It was hard to stay quiet or sad on a day like
this.

"Enjoy it while you can," said George, as the
truck turned in at the Dauphinee's driveway, "because I hear he wants another storm tomorrow.
Gale force winds and lots o' rain."

"O.K. by me," said Duncan. "We've had almost

two weeks of sun, and I'm kinda sick of it. Let's play Monopoly tomorrow in the Dauphinee's barn."

Reginald coughed slightly.

Everyone looked at him and said nothing. He looked at the floor of the truck and then at his knees. He fiddled with his shirt buttons. Then he muttered something.

"What?" No one could hear.

"I said I'm sorry about what I said. Two weeks ago. On the Government Wharf and all. I knew it wasn't true."

Nobody answered him. James dug Lorinda in the ribs, but she looked straight ahead, her face like a granite rock.

Then suddenly Jessie yelped, in a loud voice, "Reginald come, too!"

Lorinda groaned out loud. "Oh, good *grief!*" she exclaimed. "Sometimes you're so darn fair, James, that you make me sick! And don't tell me that now Jessie's getting the bug, too." She looked at Reginald for a long moment. She frowned. Then she sighed.

"Oh, all *right!* C'mon too, if you want to. Tomorrow morning at nine o'clock. In our barn. And see you don't do anything to scare Petunia and turn her milk sour."

Reginald didn't even say whether or not he'd come. And he didn't thank anyone for the ride. But they all watched as he walked off towards home. He wasn't slinking along the way he usually did. He was straight and tall, and there was a bounce in his step.

Lorinda gave James a good-natured shove. "I bet if you were a zoo keeper," she chuckled, "you'd be extra nice to the boa constrictors."

Then Mrs. Dauphinee called over her shoulder as she let Jessie in the back door. "The restaurant's open for peanut butter sandwiches!" So they all spilled out of the truck and followed her into the house.

"Some month, eh?" said Lorinda to James, as she reached for the jar of peanut butter.

"Was it ever!" said James, grinning, as he started to butter nine slices of bread. "Even though old Hank never did get to see a giant albacore. But you know what that means, don't you?"

"What?"

"It just means he's gonna have to come back again sometime." He licked some peanut butter off his thumb.

"Yeah," he said, *"Some month!"*